ACCESS

THIRTEEN TALES

Praise for *Access*

Xu Xi has a sharp ear. The dominant voices in her latest collection of short stories belong to the bold and elegant Chinese women, the high achievers, losers, dreamers, and dancers with families and lovers, who are separated by continents and cultures. Their stories, unsentimentally told, are a stimulating read.

Suchen Christine Lim, author of *A Bit of Earth*, *Fistful of Colours*, and *Rice Bowl*

This is a collection of tales with hints of Chaucer, ranging from the world of privilege to office workers and massage girls; from heavily ironic vignettes on the corporate world to edgy stories of broken lives and selfish times. What is remarkable is that there is no irritable reaching after pathos, just sharp interior monologues combined with translucent prose like thin ice, cutting in and out of frame through private feelings and public narratives. Xu Xi is a rare writer whose perspectives can shift effortlessly between personal pronouns, gender and impersonal sex. The access code to this grammar is to glean the shadow of loss lying between language and the loneliness of existence.

Brian Castro, author of *The Bath Fugues*, *The Garden Book*, and *Shanghai Dancing*

ACCESS

THIRTEEN TALES

by

XU XI

SIGNAL8PRESS

Hong Kong

Access: Thirteen Tales
By Xu Xi
(S. Komala)
Published by Signal 8 Press
An imprint of Typhoon Media Ltd
Copyright 2011 Xu Xi
ISBN: 978-988-15161-9-0
eISBN: 978-988-15161-2-1

Typhoon Media Ltd: Signal 8 Press | BookCyclone
Hong Kong
www.typhoon-media.com
www.bookcyclone.com
www.signal8press.com

Cover image: Justin Kowalczuk
(www.justinkowalczuk.com)

CONTENTS

ACKNOWLEDGMENTS

Earlier versions of the stories were published as follows:

"Access" was included in the anthology *Collateral Damage*, Silverfish Books, Malaysia, 2004; it was first published in *Carve Magazine* www.carvezine.com, January 2003.

"Agora" was published bi-lingually (Chinese/English) in *Muse*, Hong Kong, November 2010.

"Anon." was published in *Upstreet*, Richmond, Massachusetts, No. 5, 2009, and was nominated for a Pushcart Prize in fiction.

"Available" was published in the *Saranac Review*, New York, Fall 2007; it first appeared in *dimsum*, Hong Kong, Fall 2005.

"Crying with Audrey Hepburn" was included in the anthology *Manhattan Noir*, ed. Lawrence Block, Akashic Books, New York, 2006; it was later published in *Asia Literary Review*, Hong Kong, Vol. 2, 2006.

"Famine" was selected for the anthology, *2006 O. Henry Prize Stories*, Anchor Books, New York and *The Seven Deadly Sins Sampler*, Great Books Foundation, Chicago, 2009; it previously appeared in *Ploughshares*, Boston, Massachusetts, Vol. 30, No. 4, Issue No. 95, Winter 2004-'05, for which it won the journal's Cohen Award for best story; it was first published in *Overleaf Hong Kong: Stories & Essays of Chinese, Overseas* by Xu Xi, Chameleon Press, Hong Kong,

2004; a French translation was published in *N Exposant Nouvelle,* University of Quebec, Canada, Issue #1, Fall 2007.

"Iron Light" was published in *Cutthroat: A Journal of the Arts,* Durango, Colorado, Vol. 8 No. 1, Spring 2010.

"Lady Day" was serialized in a three-part bilingual (Chinese/ English) publication in *Muse,* Hong Kong, Issue 11, 2007 & Issues 12 & 13, 2008.

"Servitude" was published bi-lingually (Chinese/English) in *Muse,* Hong Kong, Issue 32, September 2009; it first appeared in *Memorious* www.memorious.org, Issue 12, 2009.

"Space" appeared in *dimsum,* Hong Kong, Spring 2004.

"To Body To Chicken" was published in *Silk Road,* Pacific University, Oregon, Spring 2008.

"Trashy Desires of Women Nearing Fifty" appeared in *Carve Magazine* www.carvezine.com, Vol. 7 No. 6, November 2006.

"The Wang Candidate" appeared in *Asia Literary Review,* Hong Kong, June 2008.

An earlier version of the collection was a semi-finalist for the Mary McCarthy Prize for Short Fiction, judged by Mary Gaitskill and a finalist for the 2010 Hudson Prize for fiction.

TALL TALES

ANON.

I T'S fifteen years, no, *twenty?* longer? before you again see
Ginny, Guenivere Martha Genari of Indiana? Illinois? Ohio?
but anyway, an "I.O.U. state," what Ginny named her origin.
Ginny, who abhorred "Guenivere," her mother's fanciful misnomer.

She is not immediately recognizable. Plumper, but in good shape
for middle age, hair stylishly cropped, unlike her long, wild locks at
M.I.T., where you all had been on the brink of technology magic,
when DOS was still innovative. Ginny is still innovative: CEO of
Filebox-iou.com (NASDAQ: FIOU), a market leader in IT storage.
Her company weathered Silicon Valley's downturn and recently made
a high-profile Indian acquisition. A darling of Wall Street. Impossible
not to follow her career.

After her presentation, you push past the throng and shout *GG!*,
her old nickname. She frowns, peers through narrow lenses, grins, and
only then do you recognize the girl.

Later, when crowds have thinned, she is still talking a mile a
minute. She shows off a photo of her son, now four, who is "incredible
at math, thank god" and then stops to ask, "And how many do you
have?" forcing you to tell and she exclaims, "Oh, I'm so sorry."

It's okay, because it's been seven years since... *he would have been
seventeen now,* you say of your dead child. Ginny grimaces. In the
almost empty hall, a tall, gangly geek saunters up, and Ginny makes
introductions. You shake hands, say, *yes, of course, Minotaur,* because
everyone knows about this designer of the elegant web labyrinth cum
search engine manager, this multi-millionaire who heads a foundation
for the advancement of sciences in schools. Ginny's second husband,
with whom she could finally procreate.

The last time you ran into her, by chance in New York, she spoke more slowly. Her divorce was over; yours hadn't yet begun—although by then, you would not say you were happily married to Lenny.

Ginny asked, "And how is the knight?" You both smiled at her reference to Lenny's real name, Lance—Lancelot, you all called him. It had been a big Camelot joke repeated *ad nauseum*, but in the context of once-forever friendships it was, and would always be, funny.

"He'll be glad to hear I visited the queen," you replied and hesitantly added. "Do you stay in touch with… Paul?"

"Him!" Ginny was shrill. "Slow death by castration would be merciful."

You exchanged contact information because you were still in the game back then, fooling with color printing technology, but also because she is your only connection to Paul who was MIA or at least no longer called you, although you didn't tell Ginny that part.

And both of you believed—you're pretty sure Ginny felt the same—that you would stay in touch, since M.I.T. wasn't all that long ago (a mere five—no, six—years), and despite Paul, even you sympathized with Ginny because everyone did. Everyone.

So how did another *nineteen* years slip by?

It is nineteen, you calculate. Less than you first thought. She is pumped up, jabbering about her industry, her company, her son. The husband catches your eye, smiles over Ginny's chatter, and it prickles discomfort: *surely not him too, not now,* beyond menopause and desire as you are, as even she must be, this alpha female, this friend you once felt sorry for.

"I'm out of cards," she says, when you ask for hers, having handed out yours. She barely glances at it, but asks what you've been up to. *Oh, this and that, color printing's moved on.* Now she looks at your card and you see a flicker of—*Does she not remember?*—*But how could that be!* You would *never* in a million years forget GG, even if she hadn't become queen of the dotcoms.

Her husband says. "Sweetheart, I hate to break things up but…"
and turns his wristwatch towards her.

"Shit! We have to do cocktails. Hey, great to see you…" and she's
gone. Just like that. You're peeved but *never mind, she* is *a big deal
now,* and trust that after the closing session tomorrow—Ginny is the
speaker—she will finish catching up with you.

Who were we back in 1978, 1979, 1980? Ginny you've met,
Paul from Connecticut, Rich from Boston, Jenni from Singapore,
Alex from Taiwan, you. A gaggle of grad school geeks. Rich came
first, enamored of DOS. Jenni had ASCII at her fingertips, and later
zoomed in on OCR. Alex programmed anything and everything late
into the night, generating cards with square holes, seeking answers
in hollows. You devoured probability and permutations, memorized
sequences, were even so brazen as to think that *you* might be the one
to solve the problem of primes. Ginny was all round brilliant, prag-
matically precise.

But Paul! Paul was *truly* special then. Our professors said so. They
paid him extra attention. Paul won awards for anything he produced
and his future was predicted to be stellar. He did it all with such
aplomb, and condescended to grace our group, brightening the skies
above us. Girls lay their bodies down for him.

Ginny fell for Paul, hard.

But first, Ginny would reform Paul, would remove him from his
girls.

We coupled, because we were young and horny. Jenni with Alex;
they now shuttle businesses and live between Singapore and Taiwan.
Rich with the oboist he married, who plays with the symphony; they
live in Boston and he is tenured at our alma mater.

Meanwhile, you found Lenny.

"Who does journalism at M.I.T.?" Paul declared when you first
brought Lenny round to meet them over beers. Ginny poked him in
the ribs, but Paul was like that then, locked into his own stratospheric
vantage point.

Lenny breathed hard. He took instant umbrage, but being an asthmatic had mastered calm to survive. He swallowed a long draught of lager, gazed down at Paul, who was a head shorter than he and declared. "I prepare for the departments of active life."

Jenni leaned forward, almost knocked over Alex's drink. "Come again?"

"In 1865, the first catalogue of M.I.T. listed three objects for the school. The second was 'to furnish a *general* education, founded upon the Mathematical, Physical, and Natural Sciences, English and other Modern Languages, and Mental and Political Science.' That, my scientific friends, was to prepare you for 'any of the departments of active life.' Hey, someone has to write about you guys someday."

Everyone laughed, except Paul. He stared hard at your scoop neck T-shirt, his eyes roving over your small breasts. *Why didn't anyone else notice?* When the laughter subsided, he murmured. "Who the fuck memorizes catalogues?" and left the table for the john.

Ginny colored, pulled herself up straight, and signaled for another beer. "Don't mind him, Lenny. Paul needs to be a prick from time to time."

Afterwards, Lenny said he liked your group, even Paul, who later bought everyone drinks. You were in love with Lenny then, before you knew he could swallow you up, before you understood that he would love you too much, way more than anyone should.

You do a little wave from your perch the next day, but Ginny betrays no signs of recognition. Yours is hardly the only Asian face here, and this is just before she has spoken, so *other things are on her mind that must be it*. Last night, you slept well in this five-star conference hotel, lodgings you cannot really afford now that there's no longer a corporate wallet. *Never mind, networking pays off.* What would Lenny say, if he knew that you were virtually broke again, reforming once again, doing your best to avoid the tables of Vegas or Reno or Atlantic City where you are far, far better known than among this gathering of calculating minds? Shake his head, undoubtedly, and sadly acknowledge, once again, your dissolute ways. *What did you think you would find here?* A job, one you might hang onto for more than a few months? Another consulting assignment to bolster respectability before the next bet?

At the podium, Ginny rises. You've forgotten how tall she is, and high-breasted, which was how Lenny once described her. *D'you think Ginny's sexy?* you asked and he replied, *Sure.* But you persisted: *Would you sleep with her?* This time, he looked up from his typewriter. *Why would I do a thing like that, honey? I'm in love with you,* as if that were all the answer you needed from your then-fiancé.

The audience hushes, and you admire her tailored suit, the color in her cheeks. She emanates good health and success. You haven't changed much since grad school except that your hair is long now because it's too expensive to have it regularly cut well. Looking younger than your years should be a good thing, but your habits—cigarettes, begun after your son's death, and bad diet when you remember to eat at all—are the real reasons you remain slender.

What would Lenny say if he were here? He no longer covers conferences, can reach the likes of Ginny with one phone call if he really wants to. Lenny has authored books, lectures at Columbia and UCLA, pronounces on the ethics of technology. When your son died, both your worlds collapsed and you never believed you would rise again. Lenny, the lapsed Catholic, returned to church. You returned to counting cards.

The probability of a nine is one in fifteen on the next hand, 75% to the first, 63% to the second. 35% clubs, 60% hearts.

The first time you whispered this, twenty minutes after watching a blackjack table in Reno, Lenny gazed at you in shock. The casino trip had been a diversion. Three months before your wedding, you and Lenny drove out after a conference in L.A. There at the tables— roulette, blackjack, craps—your mind careened off the edge, the way it tried to but couldn't quite do so at school. Lenny watched, impressed, amazed, horrified as you won ten thousand dollars within forty-five minutes.

But honey, he said afterwards when you were both drunk on champagne, *I didn't even know you'd ever set foot in a casino.* That was when you told him, *Macau,* and that your parents were professional gamblers, a detail you'd neglected to mention, your whole past being something you deliberately wiped out of existence at M.I.T. Lenny, like everyone else, thought you an orphan, raised by an aunt in Hong Kong... which was partially true (the aunt, that is), although your parents sent money (lots of it) sporadically from Macau.

It's all right, you told your fiancé after lovemaking that night, *they'll never come to America or our wedding. They barely know I'm alive.*

Ginny is starting to speak and you turn your attention back to the woman whose bridesmaid you once were.

The bridesmaid's dress had been pale pink, which did not flatter your complexion. The wedding was along the Eastern seaboard; Paul's family was old money, Lenny observed. Everyone had rooms paid for at a hotel, separate rooms if you weren't married, which you weren't, although you slept in Lenny's room each night and the chambermaid had no sheets to change in yours.

Except for Sunday morning of the day.

The wedding was held over a prolonged weekend, one that began Friday morning and ended with a late checkout Monday afternoon, to recuperate from Sunday's bash. Saturday at dusk, after the rehearsal tea, you felt a hand on your arm as you rounded the corner towards your room.

"There you are," Paul said. "I've been looking for you."

A breeze blew through the window in the hallway. The blouse you were wearing was thin and clung to your breasts. His eyes roved. "It's time we... visited, isn't it, before it's too late?" Before you knew it, he had taken the room key out of your hand and you were in his embrace.

Entry denied.

That should have been the flashing LCD.

Instead, you let Paul's perfect fingers slide against your blouse, unbutton it, helped him unhook your bra, and when you replay the moment now, some twenty-five years later, while Paul's ex-wife stands on stage speaking of RAM and DRAM, what you recall is the sensation that you and Paul fit perfectly, the way you didn't with Lenny, the way Paul surely couldn't with Ginny, who stands about an inch taller than he.

Up above, Ginny declares. "There's a bright future ahead if we take the right steps now," but what you hear is the toast she made at her wedding: *We have a bright future because we've taken the right step here, surrounded by all our wonderful families and friends,* which made everyone sigh with joy.

The audience erupts in applause. Commotion at the podium: the sponsor presents Ginny an award and a schoolgirl brings her flowers. You've wangled your way to a front table but amid all the celebratory cackling, you think this trip a waste of time. You hadn't prepared, didn't even know Ginny was featured until you arrived and finally looked at the program. This unadulterated lack of interest is no way to network. Time to forget the lure of this world to which you once belonged.

Except that you still can belong.

Conversations these past three days zinged and zanged and you held your own. You mention companies you've worked at, drop names you know, and connect the dots so that invitations unfold, people say, *give a call why don't you,* and it's up to you to follow through. All worlds are small if you flash the right passport. Yours is a little tattered, littered with a few too many border crossings, but entry here is not denied, not entirely.

That first time, the sex was quick, then slow—very, very slow. Magnificent. The way you imagined first times should be even though they never are. His skin was silk and he made no noise, unlike Lenny, who always burst triumphant and wept, overjoyed.

That first time, he ran fingers down the length of your body. "I've imagined this," he said. "You know that, don't you?"

"And now that we know?"

"We don't stop knowing, do we?"

"But how?"

"You'll find a way," Paul said.

Six months later, at your own wedding, which was far less elaborate, you arranged what you swore would be the final assignation. You disappeared to Vegas a week prior and re-appeared with enough money for the honeymoon that Lenny couldn't afford.

In that Vegas hotel room, you asked Paul why.

He lit a cigarette. "We're the top percentile. The two of us."

"Meaning what?"

"We're too intelligent for the rest of them."

"So this is arrogance? Delusion?"

"No." He squashed out the half smoked cigarette. "This just is the way it has to be," and began making love again, entered you again, the fit exact the way Lenny wasn't, the way you suspect Ginny wasn't. *But what does it mean,* you wondered afterwards, *except that this drug, this secret obsession, could potentially destroy us all?*

Paul was the best—he never was seduced by all this crap, you think, as you watch Ginny return to her seat and the chairperson rises to say last words. *And he thought you the best as well.* That recognition was seductive, like cards, like the games of chance you return to again and again. You win for a moment, become top banana, and it doesn't matter that the next throw of the dice or the next hand might plummet you back to hell. Ginny, Rich, Jenni, and Alex played the other game, the real game. They thought you did too. Paul cut his own path, which only he could afford to do, but they assumed you were one of them.

Even Lenny assumed. He loved you, didn't he, and forgave the card counting, the disappearances, the *illness, it's an illness is all, you inherited it, in your genes, not your fault.* You tried. Gamblers Anonymous. Support groups of V.I.A.s—very intelligent addicts—and listened to alcoholics, bulimics, anorexics, shopaholics, coke head-ics, and all the other *ics* of privilege who lived outwardly respectable lives. You ran back to Paul when you could, when it got too much, to Vegas or elsewhere. Not frequently though, just enough.

Paul never tried.

At his and Ginny's third wedding anniversary celebration, she caught him fucking one of their guests. Not the first time, everyone suspected, except that this exposé was humiliatingly public and impossible for her to deny. Cartoon-ish (*in the bath house*, the grapevine giggled of the Californian poolside party, *and some kid pulled open the door to get the rubber ducky and out she tumbled forward, bikini bottom down to her knees, still connected like dogs*), but everyone was pleased because by then no one really liked Paul, whose brilliant career was careening down the slopes of his profound indifference.

In the divorce, his parents sided with her. Paul called the day his divorce finalized. Lenny was out. Paul's instincts were always exact, even without prior arrangement.

"Don't do what I did," he said.

"I don't. You're the only real vice."

"And if I stop being that?"

"I don't like the sound of that." You surprised yourself with your answer and waited, hoping silence would reveal the correct permutation. "I feel bad for Ginny—I can't help it. You really, really hurt her."

"That's okay, she deserves your sympathy. I'm the lost cause."

"And me?"

"There's hope for you yet. Just play their game."

Perhaps it was sympathy for Ginny that deleted him; you can't say for sure. Paul faded from sight and you did not search too hard. Then, the baby changed everything. You fell in love with Lenny all over again because of the baby. You even stopped disappearing because of the baby.

Ginny doesn't have much time but she seems nervous as she tells you this. They have a flight to catch, she says. Her second husband is giving an interview in the hotel lobby where she and you stand to chat.

"So you and Alex are doing well?" Her eyes focus past you.

"Alex?"

"You guys are still together, right? I mean, I've read about your companies. In Singapore?"

"Not Alex. Lenny. Lancelot, remember? We broke up awhile back. You knew; I'm sure you knew."

What is it that crosses her face? Indifference? An apologetic smile as she taps her head theatrically. "Oh, right, right. Too much happening here, you know how it is."

Across the lobby, her husband is signaling, pointing at his watch.

"Listen." She backs away from you. "Been great seeing you. Call next time you're in my neck of the woods, okay?" She runs off and you are startled by the realization that no, it is not indifference at all. Trepidation. That's what it is. Ginny is afraid of you, which accounts for all the pretense and seeming lack of recognition.

"I'm not Jenni," you whisper into her wake. "Goddamn it, Ginny. You of all people *know* I'm not Jenni."

Paul had said, lo those many years ago, "The only reason Ginny asked you instead of Jenni to be bridesmaid is because she knows I think you're smart." This was on the eve of the wedding, that first time.

"Ginny," he continued, "is a coward. She'll get everything she wants, she'll have the success and money she craves, but she'll never stop being afraid."

Dusk began its descent. You sat up in bed, pulled the rumpled sheet against your breasts. "Then don't do it."

"What?"

"Don't show. Don't marry her. Run away with me instead. If your parents disown you, I'll support us at the tables. I can, you know."

He rolled over on his front. "I know you can. I've seen you play that domino card game with the other Chinese students. I've heard you also cream them at *mahjong*."

"Lenny has no idea," you say, because this was before the Reno diversion. "For a journalist, he isn't very observant."

Paul said nothing. You were both aware that dinner with everyone was in another fifteen minutes, that the lights in your room were off, that the door was bolted, that no one could find you unless you wanted them to. Finally—and even now, retrieving that memory is drawn out, slow, an eternity of silent random access—he spoke. "It's like driver's ed. My teacher used to say *Aim high while steering*. Lenny, Ginny, the rest of them, they all aim high. They steer. They watch the road. They don't do diversions."

"And us?"

"We'd crash the car. We're just passengers hitching a ride. The problem is, walking is not an option."

"That's it?"

"That's all there is."

In front of the hotel, Ginny and Minotaur Man gesticulate at a bellhop who is placing their bags in the trunk of a limo. You want to run out after her and shout, *GG! You must remember. You must. Lancelot. I'm not angry. I never was.*

Because it was Lenny who crashed the car, with your son in it, Lenny who had forgotten to belt him in (you wouldn't have), and your son bounced into the windshield and that was the end of that. The other driver was at fault. You *never* blamed Lenny, could have loved him still, but Lenny, *Lancelot mea culpa, mea culpa*, crawled back to his Catholic sanctuary. You didn't go the tables, not at first. By then, being a mother and a home-based systems consultant was enough, was plenty, while Lenny's star ascended.

Ginny Martha Genari was Catholic too.

You know the narrative. Lenny was nothing if not exact in his insistent recounting. Conference trip. A chance encounter at church. Ginny, a star by now, alone since Paul, in pain, prior to the Minotaur. Lenny alone with you since the tragedy, in pain, also a star. One drink too many that evening over dinner. Confess, confess, you *must* absolve him. Even Ginny calls, apologizes profusely, excuses your husband entirely, begs your forgiveness. Endless agonizing.

It is all too much!

What you said was, *but Guinevere and Lancelot had to be, that's all,* meaning it didn't matter, honestly it didn't, because "to forgive" seemed too almighty, too beyond your realm. Lenny shouted, *you've never understood a fucking thing* and that was truly the worst fight of your marriage and you wonder now, what would he and Ginny have said had you told them about you and Paul, which of course you never did.

So, the tables. For the relief if nothing else. When the "incurable" addict could be decently abandoned, he left, and everyone sympathized with Lenny, not you, since you no longer had the safety of motherhood, nor the saving face of a notable career.

Ginny and Minotaur are climbing into their limo. You remain in the lobby.

"Afraid?" you had said to Paul the last time you made love. "There's no reason to be afraid. Lenny will never know."

You coupled back then because you were young and desperate enough to brazen out the skydive. For Lenny and Ginny and Rich and Jenni and Alex, landing was enough. Families, parents, churches could be proud. Paul couldn't last going along for the ride, but you, couldn't you have ridden out Lenny's star? Ginny's star? All their stars?

You saw Paul once after his divorce. Not in Vegas or Reno but in a small hotel somewhere in Manhattan, which is where you lived then, before the baby, because you said you were swearing off the tables—you had promised Lenny—and didn't want to be tempted.

Paul said. "That's not what I meant. I don't care about Lenny. Leave him. Come with me."

"So you can cheat on me too?"

"I wouldn't do that, not with you."

"What makes you so sure?"

"We, together, we wouldn't have to compete, would we? We could just be."

This time, you looked at him properly. "Tell me why. For real."

"Nova. Over and out. We happened once for a brief while. That was enough."

Then he entered you, and the fit was right, but all you felt and knew of this remained unnamed, unsayable, not like the love you could say you had for Lenny, steady on the highway, headed for a destination on the map. You and Paul convulsed in silence. For a moment, that was enough. That was almost enough.

IRON LIGHT

O VER the weekend, Ida and Rand crammed in the tourist things. Gamla Stan for history, dinner up high at the Gondolen to bird-eye Stockholm. Late afternoon drinks at T/Bar, where all Rand's associates said they simply must go. *Sixty dollars for vodkas that cost less in New York? We're out of here,* he said. Perhaps, Ida suggested, his associates, misjudging Rand's American wealth, believed he liked extravagance. But what the two of them liked most, that weekend, were the doors. Everywhere they went, the doors in the city were large, wooden and heavy, and felt impenetrably solid.

Sunday night, even though it had been a couple of months since they'd last seen each other, Ida still wanted to wait on sex until her body adjusted to being with him again. Rand was, as always, understanding. What she didn't say was how her body was changing, the vagina walls thinning, so that even the idea of sex hurt.

In the morning, she woke early to find Rand already showered and dressed. Breakfast meeting, he apologized, kissing her, *but lunch at noon?* His beard, which she used to dislike, now felt sexy, a bristly imprint on her cheek. No, she did not regret this thing of theirs; she had told her sister Gina as much before the trip. Despite a lack of intimacy, she and Rand worked.

She took her time getting up. Nowhere to be before noon was irresistible luxury. Post-Thanksgiving-but-not-yet-Christmas frenzy, this week-long trip, an unexpected fiftieth birthday present. It was all perfectly timed. When Rand had called a week earlier, offering a free business class ticket—his mileage surpassed even hers—Ida had just delivered two thousand winter solstice chopstick boxes to her largest client of the year and was ready to play, which was what she told him.

"Chopstick boxes?"

"For their mother of pearl sets. My client's a Shanghai bank, and rather than Christmas gifts, they wanted something Chinese for their corporate clients. So winter solstice, which we celebrate."

"Uh huh," but she'd heard his attention stray, the way it did whenever conversation turned to that which did not especially capture his imagination. Things Chinese, for instance, or her graphic design projects. Rand Hillman was fifty-five, long divorced, childless, an architect who courted museums and historical renovations but made his nut on commercial projects, connecting developers and their money across nations. What he loved most about Ida Ching was her financial independence, and that she was the calmest, most collected woman he knew, something he said each time they made love. They had been a sort-of couple for almost five years, and after their first year, Ida had insisted he make it exclusive, the way she had since the start, and he had readily agreed.

Ida had said, "What time's the flight?"

He told her, adding, "See you at the bar?"

"Where else?"

Short-speak, the privilege of lovers. They had met at one of Newark International's airline club bars because they both were elite members of pretty much everything that made travel exclusive. After his call, she'd felt almost romantic.

Now, the still-dark blanket of morning consoled Ida, the way all that had become familiar about Rand comforted. At nine, she showered. Over strong coffee and breakfast, she considered her day, a map of Stockholm unfolded before her as a guide. It was unseasonably warm, and by noon, she had walked for over two hours in a long circle, returning to the city center and the company's apartment where they were housed.

Knut was the only person in the office next door. He was Norwegian and the junior geek, and did not look up from his computer when Ida entered. She thought him nervous. "Lunch canceled," he declared. Flashes emitted from the screen as colored lights danced across his pimply face. The accompanying noise was staccato and sharp, like gunfire. "The week's schedule is reconstructed."

"How?"

"They fly to Oslo this afternoon."

"And where is Rand?"

He screwed up his eyes, as if trying to remember. "He will call you later. You just missed him."

It was only five past twelve. Ida found it hard to believe that Rand could not have waited to tell her himself. "When do they return?"

Now he looked up, more annoyed than nervous. "I don't know."

By late afternoon, Rand still hadn't called. Ida tried his cell, but each time, the phone rang unanswered and did not roll into voicemail as it should have. She checked her email several times, but the only messages were from her Shanghai client, thanking her for a great job, and from Gina, instructing her to forget about work and "have a good, you-know-what week." Gina at fifty-four was divorced three years, and envied her sister's more-or-less regular sex, even though Ida often said Rand wasn't just about sex, to which Gina replied, *all men are.*

How concerned should she be? Most of Rand's things were still at the apartment and all he had taken was an overnight bag. His laptop was on the desk, which meant he could not be gone long. But this lack of contact was unlike him. The thing Ida loved most about Rand was that he always stayed in touch, however fleetingly.

She skipped lunch and waited till around eight before venturing out in search of food and drink. Her map cum guidebook listed Ander's Kök nearby, which proved farther than expected, uphill, off the main road. It was small and crowded, but she found an empty bar stool and settled in, pleased to find the kind of place they preferred: hip but not overly so, pricey enough to be good but not outrageous, local cuisine that embraced the world. Right after she ordered a Cabernet, her cell phone rang. Rand's number flashed.

She twisted sideways, leaned forward and covered her left ear. Her right elbow rested on the bar. "Hey stranger," she said. No reply. "Rand, I can't hear you. Rand?" Still no response.

"Disconnected?"

The male voice, from just above her head, was deep, and it took Ida a moment to register his question. He was seated next to her, appeared to be late thirties or early forties, and was the only man in the place wearing a cardigan.

"It happens sometimes," he continued. "Especially in here. Something about this location cuts off the signal."

He looked Swedish—broad-shouldered, blond, athletic—but his vaguely European accent was not Scandinavian. She could not place the oddly off-kilter tones. "Are you a regular?" she asked.

"When I come to Stockholm." His blue eyes were provocative.

She turned from his gaze back to the menu. "So what's good?"

"Everything is delicious."

The accent hinted French and he drank what looked like whiskey. Everyone else at the bar was drinking wine. She ordered a steak, because it was the least complicated, and turned back to him, trying to decide how much conversation was warranted She switched off the phone, and slipped it into her bag.

"So you're Rand's whore," he said.

Shocked, she stared at him.

His words slurred and the accent fell away. "He's told me about you."

He was drunk, she realized. The bartender said something to him in Swedish, and he smiled, dropped some notes on the bar and walked out unsteadily.

"Your next glass of wine is on the house," said the bartender, "to make up for our friend there." He gestured at the empty seat. "Rolf's harmless, but he likes to annoy our women customers. Unfortunately, he's the owner's brother."

"He startled me," she admitted.

"Don't give him another thought."

But, of course, she did. Until her steak came. It was perfect and she drank two more glasses of the Argentinean red. Her phone did not ring again that night.

In the morning, her body bristled awake, the tips of her nipples unaccountably sensitive, all of her stirred by a dry, angry lust. She sat up quickly and felt as if she were pushing away a man—not Rand, this body felt heavier, more muscular—and she knew instantly that wine, and Rolf, had invaded her sleep. In her half-wakened state, she drew open the heavy, brocade curtains. Sunlight filtered through the overcast grey. It was late, past ten.

Where was Rand? She unplugged her phone from the charger and hit redial. Again, it rang, unanswered.

Sun rays teased the sky, shafting in and out of the cloudy grey. An iron light. It glinted, disappeared, glinted again. Five stories down on the street below, the morning bustled. She rang the office, but all she got was an automated Swedish voice, incomprehensible, and she hung up before the message ended.

Twenty five years earlier, when Ida still lived in Hong Kong, she had been on a business trip to Bangkok and picked up a man. They had sex for hours in her hotel room and the next morning, she saw that he had left his sweater, a thin cotton cardigan, and she was reminded now of that man, who had been Swedish, and who looked a little like Rolf.

For the constant traveler, there is a point in the journey when the idea of order becomes irrelevant. In the shower, Ida wondered if Rand was gone forever, if she were now stuck in Stockholm, a stranger in a land where nothing was real. She should be worried, and were she to call Gina, her sister would insist she contact the police or the American Embassy. But Gina no longer went far from home in Hong Kong, where both sisters had grown up, except for the occasional trip across the border to Shenzhen, because the masseuses and dressmakers cost less than half what they did at home. The one time Gina visited Ida in New York, she complained the taxis didn't have air conditioning. Gina also had been married to the same man for almost thirty years, and would still be if he hadn't left her for the ubiquitous younger woman from China. She had three children, all grown.

There was a loud knock at the door. Ida turned off the shower, shouted "just a moment" and grabbed a robe. Knut was leaning forward awkwardly, looking sullen. One foot held open the large wooden office door. "Rand's SIM card died," he said. "He will call when he gets another one." He turned to go back into the office.

"Wait." Ida said. "When's he coming back?"

"Don't know." The door swung shut behind him.

The weather was still too warm for December, and in the streets, people peeled back layers of down and polyester, showing off bodies before winter finally forced them into hiding. That day, everywhere she went, men who resembled Rolf or the man in Bangkok—she wasn't sure which—seemed to be staring at her. That day, her body wanted Rand. Rand was tall, thin, dark-haired, with a long nose like his German mother and pale skin like his English father. He lived in Burlington, Vermont, and flew to Europe and the Middle East on business as much as forty times a year, sometimes more. When they made love, Ida sometimes wanted to forgo all life for him. Their meetings were short and unpredictable, because Ida's business took her to Hong Kong and China around six times a year, and she was often away for three weeks or more. This week would have been their longest time together.

Her cell phone beeped once, signaling a text, just as she walked into the modern art museum. *Sorry,* wrote Rand, *but b bk 4 b'day dinner enjoy city.* So, Thursday. They were to fly out Saturday. This week was turning into yet another typical Rand encounter.

She was, unusually, at the verge of hysteria. Around her, Stockholm thronged: schoolchildren and their teachers, tour groups, Christmas shoppers. A long, day-lit corridor on her left led to the exhibits. Ida was moving slowly, loopy, her eyes still on the message, and walked into a man. The collision shook her back to normal, and she apologized, embarrassed. His hand steadied her arm, "no problem, really," his voice a smile. Startled by yet another Bangkok-Rolf, she hurried off towards the right, and ended up in the museum store.

It would not do, this simply would not do, to wander around a strange city wanting to fuck. Not her. A smart, independent, successful professional, the world in her hands, no longer angry, not really. She was in a sensible relationship with a desirable man, the dream of all those sad and lonely women who wrote optimistically romantic or daring personal ads, something Ida never did. Concentrate. The here and now of the day to day was solid, unshakable. The body would be tamed.

In Bangkok that night in '79, Ida had burned with nervous energy. The trip was already a disaster; the team arrived to find their meeting cancelled, the second time their associate agency had done so. A night off in Bangkok, because they landed too late for a flight out the same evening. The men were happy and it was clear what they meant to do, especially the married ones. She begged off to be alone that night in Bangkok, unable to face another night with the boys. She was, once again, the only woman with the creative team, just as she was frequently the only woman who did not serve tea or take shorthand at meetings in other Asian cities where she regularly traveled on business. "Iron Ice" Ching, her colleagues affectionately nicknamed her. Cool. Untouchable. Clean.

After dinner, resenting the self-inflicted solitude, she had headed for the hotel bar. It was a disco, not crowded, and a Malaysian man asked her to dance. She did, the eyes of all the *farangs, gaijins, gweilos* on her. The Western men gazed, more curious than predatory, because they knew she wasn't a hooker. Ida was ambitious but angry. Asia's business was done in a man's world, which meant hostesses, bargirls, prostitutes, towards whom she chose to be blind as the men, her boss especially, racked up charges on expense accounts. Her recompense was getting facials and manicures on the company so that her trip expense reports wouldn't be too far out of line with the others. And getting desirable assignments, ones that offered the opportunities and freedom other women craved, the price of silence.

The music slowed, and she declined the next dance. The Malaysian looked disappointed. Ida did not particularly like to dance, but the hotel had no pool and the streets were too crowded to run in the evening. She needed something to settle her and whiskey was a poor substitute. Earlier that week, she had also turned down a marriage proposal—from a wealthy Hong Kong man who owned an art gallery—and now she no longer had a boyfriend. Gina called her crazy. Ida did not think she was crazy not to marry, at least not in Asia. His parents wanted grandsons, and a daughter to sacrifice herself to their dotage, the price of upward social mobility with the right Chinese family.

She was, however, crazy to be sitting at that hotel bar, alone. But an evening out in the city—hot and rancid with exhaust fumes and the proximity of too many bodies on *tuk-tuks* and motorbikes—disgusted her. Right then, she did not like being *her*—the envy of friends for an exciting life, especially her American college girlfriends, most of whom were either married or wanting to be, since the U.S. economy was still in the toilet.

The Swede sat down next to her. He was too muscular and confident to be attractive. Her now ex-boyfriend was lean and a little distracted, like Rand.

Who had he been, that Swede? Didn't matter now. Around her now, European and other tourists examined plastic pencil cases, calendars, trinkets, all the *Moderna Museet's* pricey artifacts that said *souvenir, remembrance.* Ida picked up objects absently, thinking to buy Gina a present, ideally a small thing that packed easily. Two children were tossing a flash of white in a plastic bag to each other, squealing as they raced around the store, until their father grabbed the thing in midair and said *stop.* He tossed the item back into a large, square bin.

Curious, Ida checked out the bin and picked up a snowball in a plastic bag. She squeezed it, and the resulting crunch was the feel of real snow scooped out of a high drift from someplace like Vermont, fashioned by a child's mittened hands. Intoxicated by the sensation, she squeezed again. Her first snowfall, Connecticut, freshmen year at college, Gina shaking her awake, yelling, *Hey get your coat we're going outside* and her older sister had thrown snowball after snowball at her, laughing, while around them the drifts piled higher. Ida had known then, *this was definitely not Hong Kong*, and that she had really left home at last.

What was this thing? She did not resist a third squeeze. The label said Finland. The bin was piled high with these bagged snowballs. An insane desire, to scoop a load up in her arms, and squeeze them one by one as they fell. This was the land of ice queens and snow maidens after all, even if winter was delayed. Where was—and she knew it wasn't Rand—the person to play with, to laugh with at Finnish snowballs in plastic bags, on sale for Christmas in Stockholm? She purchased two—one for her Hong Kong associate's son, who was five and had never seen snow, and one for Gina, whose laughter rang through space.

Outside, the clouds had parted and a god-like shaft gleamed wide on the water's surface. The sun was still hidden, and soon enough, darkness resumed. It was only three. Ida considered returning to the museum since she still hadn't looked at the art. Why was she here, really? A social and business network entertained her in New York, Hong Kong, Shanghai. How much did it mean to be with Rand if he was never around? And truthfully, would she willingly live in Burlington, Vermont, assuming he'd ever ask?

She needed to walk, to absorb the chilled gloom, to dissipate energies, to ascend out of this funk. Immediately, Bangkok-Rolfs were everywhere, passing her, following her, watching her. *Rand's whore*. Stop, she told herself. Drunks the world over got to you only if you listened.

Instead, Rand: *Stockholm is stunning*. A promise of beauty, to entice her along on this sudden trip. He was right, because the city offered up clean, sharp lines of aged and contemporaneous buildings, pleasingly assembled on a cluster of islets, all in an atmosphere of health and good air. She pulled out her map—open, unfold, discover, read the copy across the cover—and flipped to the last section, F, Söderman, the district Rand said he did not know well. This was the city's Bohemia and Ida thought of what the East Village once used to be, when all life had been talk of art and design, over too many cups of coffee or cheap wine, as if that were the most important thing. The "walk through the allotments," the copy read, where one-time garden lots had been given to the poor to grow vegetables. The promise of a green walkway by the water beckoned, and despite the waning light, she set out, trusting in maps and a seasoned traveler's instincts. Gina's voice: *isn't it dangerous don't you get scared,* because she wandered all over Paris, Seoul, Kuala Lumpur, Memphis, Thessaloniki, Kolkata, to out-of-the-way adventures, sometimes with little more than a single sheet hotel map as a guide. She wondered now at her impulse to keep going, staying constantly on the move somewhere, as if every new place should yield the miracle of a first, Connecticut snowfall.

A T-bana stop was nearby, although on arrival at Skanstull station, she saw she could have walked. It was not at once apparent which way to go and she wandered a little until she saw a sign for the landmark, an unpronounceable *badet,* and headed downhill. She picked up her pace, certain now she was on the right path. Bangkok-Rolf hovered. She ignored him, pushed on. The road was longer than expected, but she could see water in the distance. Soon she was at the water's edge. Sunset descended. Rand's teasing words: *vampire hour.* A chill, and she pulled her leather jacket tighter, fastening the top button, wishing she'd worn her down coat. She trod the paved path, spooked by the silence, this off-kilter dark still too early for vampires, although she wanted an owl to hoot. Surely fact trumped fiction, the real mattered more than the unreal? She picked up her pace, barely seeing the allotments along the water's edge, wanting on the one hand to see someone come toward her yet hoping, on the other, that she could forge ahead alone.

Sex with the Swede had been violent, athletic, gymnastic against walls, on counters, the floor, racing through the positions of the Kama Sutra in a yogic decathlon. It had cleansed all anger out of her as afterwards they collapsed, laughing. Post sex had been civilized, courteous, an exchange of business cards without personal phone numbers, knowing they need never meet again. Eminently forgettable till now.

Nothing like sex with the man she should have married according to Gina, or with Rand.

She walked faster, almost a jog, as desire, or something akin, collided with the cold. In her world back in Bangkok, desire had been everything. If you could tap into the unspoken need, meet it with a promise, your ad campaign would influence people and even win awards, as several of hers did. False promises, creating need where none previously existed. It was why she finally packed up her art supplies and left, choosing the simplicity of design over the larger fiction of desire. That world had been too much for her, too messy, a passion fruit ice cream swirl when vanilla was all she wanted. Design was about clean lines, functional forms, making the imagined real. In her world around Bangkok, she occupied a stable, even enviable perch from which she could have flown to the skies, as long as she was impervious to the Asian way of doing business, of being a woman, of living life. Iron Ice, frozen despite the heat, an anomaly under the tropical and sub tropical sun.

And then, so rapidly she could barely catch her breath, here she was, days away from fifty, an independent contractor with a small New York-based business, with one sister, two nieces, a nephew, assorted extended family around the globe, a steady if occasional lover. Jogging in Stockholm. Remembering a forgettable Swede.

Who should she tell her life to? Rand?

Rand's voice: *Design is about beauty.* Rand no longer designed, assigning that privilege to his staff of talented young architects, managing the firm's profitability instead. When Rand lusted, it was over stunning photographs and images, the silhouette of the Flatiron against the cold light of Manhattan's almost-dawn. His eyes desired and she knew that his pleasure arose from seeing her wear beautiful colors or shapes, a pleasing new hairstyle, a piece of jewelry, and his gifts—he was generous in absentia—were always perfect. *Buildings speak to you if you let them,* he said, and she felt it too as they devoured cities and skylines with their eyes. But their voices, like his, only hovered in memory, did not claw at her insides or stir the depths of desire. Beauty was safe. Truth bumped up against you, sticking its ugly nose where it did not belong.

Auntie what's a whore? Her youngest niece, once, eavesdropping on their gossip, and Ida and Gina had roared with laughter but that was back when there was a brother-in-law and a happier family.

The path was longer than imagined from her map, and still empty, and in the darkness, she became afraid. Not, as she told herself, of the dark or the strange land, although she felt a slight apprehension. It was the absence of anything real. There was her cell phone, but how real was that when she could not recall the international code for Sweden, she suddenly realized, the code she needed to call anyone here. The trees loomed over this gothic fairy tale walkway as every troll and mythical creature danced before her. No vampires though. It wasn't the right country, surely. But a wolf or Loki could appear and whisk her to some Nordic forest where she might be lost forever. Rand did not know Söderman, despite his familiarity with Stockholm. If she stopped and walked off the path into the river, no one would find her for days.

Stop being morbid, she told herself. These stories you told children had nothing to do with her, now, turning fifty, her vagina drying as she jogged. Rand was understanding, a man of this post-feminist, post-psychological, post-mortem modern age, who did not dwell too long in emotional muck. Some doors you kept shut.

Her cell phone beeped. The text said, *hey u bk 2nite;).* She stopped, texted back to ask what time. *8,* he said, *wear sunrise ok?* and she knew Rand had sex on his mind. Sunrise was the gray with the pale orange scarf, the dress that slid off easily the night he said, *We work, you and I, don't we.* It had not been a question. These unexpected schedule changes were typical of Rand's work, of Rand's life. At least he had made the effort to return, so that they could have the week together as planned. She shrugged back, *sure,* and his response startled her: *tks 4 for ur patience.*

How much longer was this path? Four thirty now and the dark had settled in completely. The river flowed steadily, no surges or roars, no sluggish, murky depths. Bangkok-Rolf had surprised her with his gallantry. *I didn't hurt you, did I?* he had asked, and even though she felt some pain—how could she not after all those unaccustomed acrobatics—she shook her head, smiled, said no and thanked him for his concern. They had been civil, just as she and Rand remained always civil in their passions. Worked better that way. There had been a few odd men after Bangkok-Rolf, not many, and those were best forgotten. She had dated a couple of other men, one seriously enough for awhile, but then work took over, life in New York was pleasurably social and busy, then her parents died, one right after the other, then she met Rand, then her sister divorced and that despair thrummed for a time. It was a life like any other, some moments more painful than others, and Rand was on the continuum that did not shatter expectations.

She pressed ahead, conscious of the time, the reality of a schedule strangely calming. The body was a miraculous thing and sex only painful if you said it was. Otherwise the discomfort passed, and you moved on. The last time she saw her gynecologist, she was told it might be helpful to consider a topical estrogen cream. Then, the dryness had not been as acute.

A ringing bell from behind alerted her. Hi, the cyclist said, as she pedaled past Ida. Ahead of her, a couple were walking down the path and she stopped them, asked how much further it was to the next station. Twenty minutes, he said, half an hour, she said, and then they looked at each other and laughed. Ida felt her cheeks flush as she jogged ahead, determinedly now. The chill was gone and the air was invigorating as her limbs awoke to the constant movement. The garden plots she passed were not in bloom, but everywhere she looked, she saw signs of life in another season. The tied-up boats. The covered outdoor furniture. These small houses lined the shore, like guard posts, marking the historical path of sustenance for the poor, this path that was a respite from the city, a green detour for weary souls. The minutes ticked as she wound her way. Civilization ahead, soon.

THE WANG CANDIDATE

SHE was "not fat, hardly" but "acceptably buxom," Millicent Parsons said of the job candidate, oblivious to the political incorrectness of her remark. What Miss Parsons meant was that she had decided Lei-li Chen was going to be their new circulation and subscriptions manager and that no further discussion was needed.

After the staff meeting, Ashley slumped her svelte back against the publisher's closed office door, further baring her midriff. "Ted, this is *insane*. Why on earth should Parsons have any say? You *know* Eric's way better, *and* he can copy edit. You *know* this Chinese woman can't." She was the journal's "assistant editor" of two months, a recent Sarah Lawrence graduate and Ted's latest crush. Eric was Ashley's latest fling.

Ted smiled. "You're magnificent when you're angry, you know that?"

She scowled. "Don't even."

Ted said, "Look, that's Parsons's area. She's been doing it forever and knows what she wants." His eyes fixed on Ashley's navel ring. "You're here to move us onto the web and all that good stuff, but until that happens, we still need to do things the old way and Eric will..." but he was interrupted by a coughing fit.

Ashley straightened up. "You're too old to be smoking," she said, and left.

Ted Wright gazed after, wondering how much longer she would hang around. The last one—Georgetown, smarter but less confident than Ashley—stayed half a year before succumbing to a Ph.D. Whenever Ted thought about leaving the journal, yet another young, pouting vision would flit across his path and for a little while he could recall the sweetness of love-lust. Besides, fifty-eight was "not old, hardly," as Millicent frequently pointed out. Dear cousin Millicent: at seventy-five she still labored unpaid as "executive secretary," reluctantly conceding the addition of "executive" five years before at Ted's insistence. She had never taken a salary in the fifty-five years of the journal's existence. The journal owed everything to her. It was how she chose to spend the money that had come from her mother, a rather glamorous foreign correspondent who'd died in the Second World War, a foreign correspondent from a rich family of brewers. Her father was already in poor shape when that happened and she spent the next twenty years looking after him until his liver finally gave out. Millicent was, of course, nothing like her mother who would have dumped her husband in a nursing home, or so family gossip went. The journal in those years was a balm for her, but her name never appeared on the masthead—it was the way she preferred to do things—and few readers had heard of her or knew that the publisher and editor-in-chief, cousin Ted, was in any way related to the foundation that funded the journal, and therefore, his life.

**

Worldly Affairs: A Journal of Political Economics was entrenched as an institution among the "international intelligentsia," as Ted sometimes called his readers, not always reverently. It came out twice a year, it had 300-plus pages to an issue, and it continued to grace the shelves of government offices, university libraries, and social science departments despite the coming of the Internet and gradual collapse of other similar journals whose demise Millicent derided as "inevitable due to their lesser significance." What she didn't know, because Ted never told her, was that he kept the subscription price uncommercially low and gave away as many copies as the rules governing audited circulations would permit. Profit, unlike a wide readership, was not a necessary outcome of the endeavor, but business and business-like methods mattered to Millicent and combined in her mind

to mean only one thing: the Wang computer. The acceptably-buxom
Lei-Li had a good degree in politics and economics from Shanghai's
best university; her CV showed she'd worked hard in the nine years
since; but the Wang was the real reason she got the job.

The Wang was an old workhorse, installed a year before Ted
took over, during the era known as "Bob's time." Bob was Robert B.
Smithers, a Brit and a former *Financial Times* correspondent, who was
really interested only in what he called 'the inky end' of the business,
by which he meant editing pieces and taking potential contributors
for long lunches where they discussed, or so he always alleged in his
expenses, features on the South Korean economy or After Gorbachev,
Who? The lunches eventually paid off—he got a lucrative job commis-
sioning reports for a big Wall Street investment bank—by which
time Millicent was firmly in charge of all the things Bob neglected:
renewal rates for subscribers, circulation reports, stock levels, back-
number orders. Once, all this information had been collected and
collated in ring-binder folders and indexing cards that Millicent's
fingers would ripple through. The Wang abolished them. Ronald
Ho, software consultant and former Wang programmer installed the
system. Unlike Bob (the former publisher's choice), Ronald Ho was
Millicent's find, and consequently the Wang became her pet. She
even gave it a name, Lily. What she denied, or so Ted believed, was
that Lily was the love surrogate for Ronald.

Lily was brilliant, Millicent claimed, because no matter what new
variable had to be added to any of their distribution lists, all she had
to do was type in the new information and "she spits out what we
need," meaning circulation reports, mailing inserts, coded subscription cards, sorted mailing lists, and labels for seminar and conference
distribution. "Even a complete novice at computers like me can use
it," Millicent would say. She went on saying this when faster and
more sophisticated systems replaced Wangs everywhere else, because
Ronald appeared at Millicent's command to service and effect all
necessary re-programming. An efficient and willing slave.

On the first Friday in April, 1994, a crisis.

One day earlier, Ronald Ho had dropped dead of a heart attack right in their office while servicing the Wang. Ted was sure Millicent would suffer a nervous breakdown. Meanwhile, a major conference in Geneva loomed, and that day was the shipping deadline for a few boxes of the complimentary copies that were being sponsored by *The Economist*. Around 2:30, Millicent marched into Ted's office, where he was with the new sales rep from their printing company, their heads nearly touching as they examined an array of cream-colored paper stock samples, fanned out on Ted's desk.

"Lily simply won't spit today," Millicent declared. "What are we going to do?"

The sales rep backed away and lost her balance, landing against the arm of the old sofa that lay next to the desk.

Ted stood up. "Are you all right?"

Millicent banged both hands on the desktop, sweeping aside the arc of cream. "Ted, pay attention. This is more important than your libido."

The young woman blushed and attempted to gather her samples. "Millicent, really..."

"Ted, *Lily*. We're talking *Geneva*."

The rep was leaving. "Please..." Ted began, but the woman escaped. He glared at Millicent. "Now are you satisfied?"

"Honestly Ted, she's barely pubescent. Besides she's not nearly anorexic enough for you. But never mind her. How will we get the labels done? Can't you call Wang? They're in Lowell, aren't they? Someone can get here in time if he leaves right away." She seemed to Ted almost in tears.

His tone softened. "Dear heart, the company's bankrupt and they've just auctioned off their headquarters." He hesitated before adding, "Ronald was..."

Millicent banged his desk again, this time alarming Ted. Her face was hard. "Forget Ronald! He's gone. But there must be *someone* who can help. This is *Geneva*."

Shaken, Ted tried to think. Cousin Millicent was, as usual, tougher than she seemed. Millicent was also right: Geneva was too important to screw up. Besides, he was looking forward to this trip for two reasons. In the new year, GATT would be replaced by the WTO, so the buzz and gossip would be riveting. More important, the brilliant and sensual Andrea Trenton would be there, recently separated from her husband; if he got her tipsy enough, she could be this conference's fling. Luckily the current intern, a surly Goth, just happened to have a daddy who worked for the *Economist*. She was asked to ring Daddy and ask him to intervene with the marketing director, to explain that their sponsored copies would be a day or two late. The Goth grimaced, wrinkling her fearsome make-up—was this kind of thing the work of editorial interns?—but obliged.

Millicent worked through the night typing the names and ranks of more than a thousand delegates while Ted peeled the labels that came off her typewriter and stuck them to more than a thousand copies of the magazine. On his way home just before dawn, under a waning gibbous moon, Ted felt certain he was finally done with the Wang. By Monday afternoon, he'd placed his order for the long-desired PC circulation and distribution software—the same program successfully used by numerous publications nationwide but rubbished repeatedly by Millicent—and contracted a technical consultant to set up a new system that very week. The PC and printer were installed, Millicent and the intern were duly trained in their use, and the latter became noticeably cheerier (as Goths go, that is), embracing the new system as if it were her own.

Three months passed, a new Goth replaced the old, and Ted went on his annual summer vacation to the Vineyard with the now-divorced Andrea Trenton, the eminent political scientist and latest contributor to the journal; since Geneva, she had regularly raised more than Ted's spirits. When he returned, he stopped in to chat with the new intern, a tall, emaciated guy from Reed whose name Ted would never quite say, but who was Andrea's only child. He was surprised to see the kid churning out labels from Lily. Millicent was out that day, running errands.

"Why are you using the Wang?"

The Goth shrugged and waved at the PC. "Not working."

"What's wrong with it? Did you call our tech support?"

"Been and gone. Said we need a new one."

"But this system's brand new!"

The Goth glared, then yawned. The silver bone that was pierced through his tongue clinked against his incisor.

Ted never got a satisfactory answer from his consultant, who claimed that the PC had been damaged irreparably; "someone" had scrambled the innards and the software disks were scratched. All Millicent would say was that one morning the system wouldn't work so she went back to Lily because there was a job to be done. The Goth shrugged, but Ted couldn't help noticing that he and Millicent seemed to get along famously, and when he left, she gave him a Che Guevara T-shirt as a going-away present and he gave her an enormous hug, which Ted considered un-Goth-like in the extreme. Lily, meanwhile, soldiered on, and Ted withdrew, defeated. The PC and printer sat in their offices, gathering dust, until they too became obsolete.

That was the story of the Wang according to Ted.

**

A week after Lei-li's interview, Ted rang her in New York to give her the job.

"Shall we say, in two months? Will that be enough time for you to move?"

She was still reeling from her unexpected good fortune. "Oh, sure, sooner if you like. I'm quite flexible."

Ted thought of the young woman's face—well, not *that* young, really. She had surprisingly full lips. "No," he replied, "two months is fine. Subject to your references checking out of course, but I'm sure that's no problem." Later, Ted wondered if he weren't making a mistake, caving in to Millicent so readily.

What no one had noticed was a typo in Lei-li's resume. *Wong Enterprises,* read the section under **Current Employment**:

Finance and Administrative Manager for an international import-export company with operations in New York, Hong Kong, and China. Responsibilities include overseeing the Wang computer system inventory software...

She had meant *Wong.* The company was her uncle's and her cousin had programmed the software and trademarked it with the family name.

Millicent had jumped on that *Wang,* and placed Lei-li's resume at the top of the pile. It wasn't that Millicent insisted—Millicent didn't *insist*—but Ted saw the potential for fury if he crossed her on this one. The last time he felt that wrath was over Andrea, when she left him.

It hadn't been his fault, *hardly,* but single mothers were testy about their children, and perhaps he had been a tad insensitive to gripe as often as he did about the kid's work habits, or lack thereof. And perhaps it might have helped if he had called him more often by name, but honestly, *Payton?* It had been two years since their wonderfully salacious encounter in Geneva. Their continued relationship surprised him: he hadn't expected much beyond the conference. For Ted, it was two blissful years, more satisfying than anything he'd experienced since perhaps his twenties. Andrea was coming to the end of her two-year term as a visiting scholar at Harvard, and Ted had visions of regular cross-country trips to her home in Seattle. They'd just had sex at his place and Ted was about to light a cigarette.

She eyed his lighter. "Could you take that outside, please?"

"Dear heart, it's frigid out."

"Then wait."

"Till when? It's not like I'm headed home." He smiled and traced the cigarette over her right breast.

She flicked it away from her nipple. Shreds of tobacco flittered her skin. "Stop that."

He took her reasonably ample breasts in both hands and leaned forward to kiss them, but she held him off.

"Ted, stop. We have to talk."

And that was when Andrea broke it off, amid his protests. Finally, round about five the next morning when she, exhausted, could no longer take his arguments, and he demanded for what must have been the twentieth time, *it's your son, isn't it, he's never liked me,* and she was tired of telling him it wasn't true, because Payton actually found Ted *a riot and a half Mom so when's he moving in he can have my room as a study and you guys can pay to set me up in an apartment, no big deal,* Andrea finally said, "Ted, you're just too old for me," which shut him up, as she hoped it would.

In recounting their break-up to Millicent the next day, Ted could not understand why she seemed so fidgety.

"I'm only seven, no eight years her senior. That's not too old. It's an excuse... and Millicent, *what* are you doing?"

His cousin was rearranging the globe and ashtray on his desk, sliding them to the left, then forward, then to the right.

"This is all wrong Ted, can't you see? Completely wrong. It's always been wrong."

"For god's sake, Millicent, will you stop that and listen to me?"

She stopped and glared. "You're so damned privileged, Ted. Always have been."

Her tone startled him. "What on earth are you talking about?"

She stood up and Ted thought she had never looked more ferocious. "You're a complete idiot, you know that? An insensitive, self-centered, amazingly obtuse idiot. No wonder you never married. Andrea was way too good for you."

"But *she's* the one who..."

But Millicent had already left, slamming the door with such force that the ashtray shivered.

The memory of Andrea unsettled Ted—he hadn't thought of her in a long while—and he turned back to the contract for Lei-li. Millicent had been edgy for days, annoying him hourly, until he agreed to hire her. As he signed the document, he recalled that when he left her at the bus station for the trip back to New York, she had lit up the instant she was out of the car and inhaled with such a look of relief as if to say, *thank god that's over.* It occurred to him that Millicent probably didn't realize Lei-li smoked. The thought tickled him.

The day Lei-li started at *Worldly Affairs,* Ashley quit. She and Eric were off to Tokyo to teach English.

"Why don't you take Ashley's office?" Millicent said before Ted could object. "It's much more spacious and you'll be near the Wang."

Lei-li settled in, pleased with her new environment. The move to this small New England town from Queens, New York had been less difficult than she expected, and already her new apartment felt like home. She placed a photo cube on her desk with the picture of her dead parents facing her. The other three shots were of friends in Shanghai, the city she'd left nine months ago after her parents were killed in a bus crash in their hometown in Fujian province. Her mother's only brother, an importer of preserved pickles, frozen dumplings, and other necessities, shuttled his business and family between Hong Kong and Queens. He had insisted Lei-li come to New York, live with his family, and get a green card. Originally, she jumped at the opportunity but had since come to regret that decision.

This job, however, was the advent of a new life, one she could direct on her own, away from her relatives' judgments.

When she informed her uncle she was moving, he had shouted. "You're going *where?* Are you crazy? What will you do for groceries, or if you need help? There won't be any Chinese there."

She continued tapping the keyboard, inputting the figures of her uncle's latest inventory. "I want to make money."

"We don't feed you? You don't earn enough to spend here?" Her uncle's Mandarin slid, tonally, towards Cantonese.

"I mean my own money. And I want my own place." She glanced up at the photo of her parents on the altar table, wondering what they would think of their resting place on this Buddhist artifact. Neither of her parents had been religious. "I've imposed on your family for too long already," she added, hoping to mollify him.

Her uncle turned apoplectic. "My sister... you... what kind of... *aiyaah! Neuihyan gaam dou yauh gah?*"

The phone rang, and Lei-li answered. "It's Mr. Cheung," she said, holding her hand over the mouthpiece. "He wants to know if you have any fish balls."

"How many boxes?"

"Six dozen."

Her uncle nodded, calmer now that he could shift gears back to business, where things were straightforward. Young nieces from China, on the other hand, complicated his life more than even the most incomprehensible sutras.

Lei-li was grateful for the interruption. As far as she was concerned, this was a done deal, regardless of what womanly protocol her uncle thought she violated. Mother, unlike her uncle, had been of a calmer disposition, and had not opposed her remaining in Shanghai after university. How she had loved Shanghai! And the work opportunities. So many for graduates who knew some English; even her classmate who had practically failed English got a highly paid job with an American exporter. Lei-li's last position had been as an advertising ﹏nd circulation sales manager for an international business weekly. At thirty-two, she earned more than her father ever had and lived in an apartment with its own private toilet.

But today, her uncle was as forgettable as the last emperor. This job paid *real* money, unlike the pittance her uncle doled out; soon she'd have enough for a ticket back to Shanghai.

Around 3:30, Ted Wright stopped by. "So, how's Lily?"

"No problem." Lei-li had long ago discovered that Americans loved this response. In fact, Lily was nothing like the last system she used in Shanghai, which was compatible with the latest Microsoft Windows. This program was ridiculously constrained, one that required an inordinate amount of manual intervention. Scraps of paper with code references and other reminders littered the bulletin board next to Lily, just as details about how everything ran (like their advertising sales rep's phone number or their accountant's name and address) were always in someone's head, rather than recorded in any organized or accountable fashion. But this convolution was similar to the way her uncle ran his operations which, given the newness of life right now, was just fine.

He frowned. "What a pity. Well, I'm gone for the day. Tell Millicent please."

Millicent was in the toilet again. Lei-li couldn't help noticing that Miss Parsons spent a large part of her days closeted there. *Worldly Affairs'* offices comprised the garage, which was mainly storage, and the basement level of Millicent's home, a magnificent Victorian house. The publication's premises were the only parts of the house that staff were permitted to enter, but during her first couple of weeks, Lei-li peered into the windows of the first floor several times from out back by the garage when Miss Parsons and Ted weren't around. Including herself, the entire staff consisted of five people plus, of course, Lily. Ashley had vacated one post and the other was for an intern. Since it was just the beginning of summer, the latest intern had yet to arrive. Lei-li's job was a newly created position and for a time she was the sole employee.

On her first day, Lei-li worked till five, walked back to the apartment, and made herself a light supper of tofu and rice, seasoned with ginger and sesame, all of which she'd acquired at the local food co-op. She spent the evening reading quietly, which had been difficult to do in Queens. It wasn't like Shanghai, where friends stopped by or rang her to go out and where something was happening all the time and she had more money than she could spend, even after sending her parents their share. But this felt like home, the way it had been when she was a girl, among the books her parents reinstated long after their "rehabilitation," and life could go back to what it used to be once the revolution was past.

Ashley proved difficult to replace. Only young men showed up to be interviewed. Even the new intern was some guy from John Hopkins. It was not that Ted Wright *consciously* chose the stream of pale, anorexic young women, hardly, but he believed in indulging tender, and *harmless* if he might say so himself, crushes. Besides, the journal functioned with or without an underpaid "assistant editor" since Ted was highly competent and smart about paying real editors, freelance, to do the bulk of the work in much the way he farmed out advertising sales, warehousing, accounting, and graphic design. At fifty-eight, despite Millicent's accusations, Ted's libido did not rage. It had raged with Andrea, and also, when he was nineteen, with a magnificently endowed stripper who bore his child, a girl he'd never seen. Millicent, bless her, had paid off the woman to disappear, without a word to his parents, now both deceased. Ted suspected Millicent provided child support afterwards but she never said and he never asked.

Meanwhile Lei-li was working out, it seemed, and got along with Millicent and Justin, the latest intern who, thankfully, actually *liked* proofreading and was good at it.

Two months after Lei-li joined and an assistant editor still had not been found, Ted invited her to lunch.

He took her to Sasha's, the one nice place in town, although technically, it was just outside the border of the township, some ten miles away from town hall.

"Guess what," Lei-li said when they'd been seated. "There's a Sasha's in Shanghai too, a real fancy place. I've only been once. It's where the foreign correspondents meet."

Ted opened the menu. "How droll." Foreign locales (although he made an exception for Washington, DC and, formerly, Geneva) did not intrigue him; his European tour as a young man had put him off travel for its own sake, and to date, he had managed to miss China, although that was fast becoming unavoidable. What worldly sophistication he possessed, which was considerable, was derived from his intellect and stomach.

"So what's good?"

"Everything." Ted closed the menu. He wished she weren't quite so chirpy.

After their waiter departed with the order, Ted asked. "So you like being here? You're settling in okay?"

"It's a very challenging job. I'm learning all the time."

"Excellent. And you like working with Millicent?"

"Miss Parsons," because this was how Millicent preferred to be addressed, "is very knowledgeable." She paused while the waiter set down her juice and his wine. "And kind."

Ted tasted the New Zealand Pinot Noir, a new selection on the by-the-glass list. Reasonable. "She can be kind," he said. "What about Justin?"

"He's very nice, and helpful."

"And Lily?"

He was pleased to see her crack the faintest glimmer of a smile. "As Miss Parsons says, Lily is loyal and earns her keep."

"Excellent." He stared at her and took another swallow. Strange how at home she seemed, given how little time she'd actually been here. She had checked out fine, references and all—he was nothing if not duly diligent—but Ted still couldn't help wondering how someone like her lived, alone, without connections or family, with only this job as an anchor.

Their food arrived, allowing a reprieve from conversation; she had followed his lead and ordered the *blanquette de veau*. He found the entire occasion uncomfortable, which was unusual, because restaurants were generally where Ted felt most at home. A gourmet palate was the real reason he succumbed to travel, that and enforced attendance at numerous conferences. Yet he carried his food and drink easily, having only a very slight paunch, and did not look ridiculous in his well cut and rather expensive clothes.

By his second glass—usually he confined himself to one at lunchtime—he was pleasantly buzzed and less uncomfortable. He sneaked a glance at her figure. Millicent was right; she *was* acceptably buxom. Like Andrea.

Lei-li asked. "Will you hire an assistant editor soon? It must be difficult to manage everything yourself, when you're so busy, I mean."

Ted was still fixated on Andrea, and was surprised to find himself aroused. He drank some water, swallowing a small piece of ice. "I expect so."

"You know," she began slowly. "Justin..."

Sasha appeared at that moment, glanced at Lei-li, and stopped to chat with Ted, who proclaimed the Pinot Noir *not bad, not bad at all*, grateful for the distraction. Lei-li waited, and Ted noted that for a young woman, she seemed surprisingly patient. But of course, she wasn't "an infant," as Millicent described the Ashleys of the world, and her dress and demeanor struck him as those of someone older.

"As I was saying," Lei-li continued a few minutes later, "Justin has a friend who needs a job. He's finished his master's at John Hopkins."

"Really?"

"By coincidence, he's visiting right now."

Ted smiled. The veal was particularly well prepared today and the reminder that his libido still functioned, despite the lack of recent use, was reassuring. "I suppose I should meet him then, don't you think?"

"I'll arrange it," she replied.

Justin's friend Brandon Chang joined *Worldly Affairs* two weeks later and Lei-li found every excuse to stop by his office. He was American born, from Baltimore, and had an open friendliness and charm she found irresistible. Often, he would pat her shoulder or back lightly when they spoke and Lei-li had to suppress the desire to throw herself at him, literally, because the feeling of him filled her bed at nights. It was almost a year since there'd been a man to sleep with and she woke up most mornings moist with wanting.

The Tuesday morning before the Baltimore conference, Millicent went into the bathroom at around ten fifteen. By ten forty-five, she still had not emerged. A loud-ish thump sounded. Lei-li grabbed the spare skeleton key which Miss Parsons hung on a hook by her desk and unlocked the door. The seventy-six-year-old woman was slumped on the floor, her cotton underwear around her knees. At the hospital, the doctor immediately diagnosed a severe case of hemorrhoids, one that "should have been treated *years* ago. How the hell did she endure this?"

Late in the afternoon, Justin remarked. "That explains the case of Preparation H in the closet." He and Brandon were trapped between sympathy and a grim hilarity.

Ted glared at the boys, but he was thinking that Millicent's diet was to blame, the *way* she ate, so badly and unbalanced. The four employees of *Worldly Affairs* sat together in Ted's office. Lei-li repeated, for what must have been the twentieth time, "Poor Miss Parsons," unable to dispel the shock of her initial discovery. Hemorrhoids did not amuse her, having once suffered herself as a child, a result, the doctor told her mother, of sitting too long on the chilly *kang*—her stone bed that doubled as a furnace—because the price of fuel had been outrageous that winter and the family was scrimping.

"Time for a drink," Ted declared, uncorking a bottle of Cabernet. "The point is, what are we going to do?"

It transpired that nothing was ready for the Baltimore conference. Justin had been working on Atlanta, two months hence, and Lei-li was wading through the mire of annual subscription renewals, a hangover from Millicent's refusal to abandon yearly ones in favor of the two-year and five-year terms Ted wanted. Ted had been concentrating on the next issue, which was only two weeks away from printing. Only Brandon had the vaguest notion of Baltimore, because he had been charged with writing Ted's remarks.

Brandon said. "We never discussed the proofs for the next issue." Ted drank half a glass quickly and nodded. "I know."

"Perhaps," Lei-li began, "Brandon should go to Baltimore and give Ted's remarks. He knows the city well and has contacts there. And maybe Justin as well. To make up for the issues that weren't sent, and Ted not being there, Justin could man a table, give away issues, and collect names for subscription mailings. What do you think?"

The three men turned their gaze towards her. Brandon smiled, Justin grinned, and a spark lit Ted's eyes.

Ted said. "Lei-li, that's a sound idea."

"I called the organizer and explained we had a medical emergency. They're waiting for me to call back and let them know what we're going to do."

"Call them," Ted said.

They all worked late that night, and when he left, Brandon gave her quick hug. "Thanks Lei. This is such a terrific opportunity for me, you have no idea."

"No problem," she replied, but afterwards, her breasts were tender, and that night she dreamt of this younger man's body pressed against hers, and then he was above her, behind her, wrapped tightly around her, fucking her till she swooned.

In the morning, Ted was already in the office when she arrived at eight. "It's just you and me, kiddo." The premises were a mess. Empty wine glasses, a disarray of papers, partially printed label rolls, half-packed boxes, all the leftovers of a hurriedly arranged affair to prepare Brandon and Justin as representatives of *Worldly Affairs*. Lei-li began tidying up, and by nine thirty the offices were in order again. Ted popped over to the hospital in the afternoon and when he returned, she asked, "How is Miss Parsons?"

Ted sighed and gestured for her to follow him into his office, where he slumped behind his desk. "She's under sedation. They have to operate." He was shaken, having finally absorbed the enormity of the trouble he faced now that the immediate emergency was over. "Luckily, she's strong as a horse. The doctor thinks she'll do fine."

Lei-li stood by the door in silence.

He looked up without really seeing her. "She's always been there, you know. For years. I never thought..." and suddenly, he began to weep silently, his whole body heaving rhythmically, punctuated by the wheeze of early emphysema. Tears rolled down his face, and for once, he did not concern himself with either appearance or propriety.

She went to him and placed a hand on his shoulder. "Please don't worry, Ted. Miss Parsons will be all right."

He gripped one of her arms and stared up at her. "You don't understand. Hardly anyone knows this, but she's my cousin, my only blood relative in the world." He spun his chair round to face her and grabbed onto her other arm. "Things change all the time. Hell, all the world does is change, but the big affairs of state, they don't really matter, do they? But this. I just never thought... never had to."

Her arms were beginning to hurt, and Lei-li was embarrassed by the awkwardness of her position. He kept tugging, and the force was so great she finally gave in and stooped down in front of him. He raised her arms so that they lay on his lap, pulling them forward so that her hands encircled his waist.

"Ted, please let go."

Instead he leaned forward and embraced her, raising her up against his seated self until she fell into his lap. He seemed barely conscious of what he was doing as he groped her breasts, pushing one of her hands against his cock, which was harder than it had been in a very long while. He was not especially tall, but now, as he stood them both up, he seemed to tower over her. He held her firmly in his embrace and walked them towards the couch. He reached under her skirt, which was fitting but not tight, and his fingers sought the damp warmth. Despite herself, Lei-li pulled at his fingers, forcing them deep inside her.

When they awoke, it was dark out. Lei-li sat up first. Her skirt and panties were around her ankles. She still had on her jacket, although her blouse was unbuttoned to her navel and her bra was unhooked. Ted was completely naked. She saw his clothes torn and scattered around the floor, and recalled that she had ripped at his shirt and undressed him with a fierce urgency. He blinked, sat up slowly, took stock of the situation, and said, softly, "Ahh, shhhhiiiitttt." Then, as

Lei-li got dressed and he covered himself, he added, "This is dreadful. I'm so sorry."

He peered around vaguely and Lei-li reached over to his desk. Her hand found the pewter paperweight globe in the dark, and she located his cigarettes next to it.

She held them out to him. "You want these, right?" He nodded. "I should go home now?"

"Wait. What time is it?"

"Very late."

"Perhaps you should stay in the spare room. Millicent keeps it made up." He pulled his boxers out of the heap and put them on. Taking her hand, he led her to the interior stairs leading to the first floor. "Come on, it's okay, really," because she hesitated at the foot of these stairs, which she had not ascended since her arrival at *Worldly Affairs*.

"Miss Parsons might not like it?"

Ted smiled. Lei-li's deference to Millicent reminded him of his own when he had been younger. In between breaths, her lower lip vanished and reappeared, vanished and reappeared, and her lips looked swollen and lush, like overripe fruit. Despite himself, he leaned forward and kissed them. She backed away—sobered now, he assumed, by her explosive orgasms. It had been awhile since he'd tangled so hard with a woman. Not since Andrea.

"Come on." He coaxed her up the stairs. "You don't have anything to worry about. Really."

Brandon and Justin returned, euphoric, four days later, and Lei-li realized something she hadn't noticed before: Brandon physically resembled her old boyfriend. He seemed much younger to her now, almost juvenile, and for the first time, she focused on the fact that he was seven years her junior. His presence in the office was no longer troubling. Around Ted, she was not sure how to act, but he carried on in an ordinary manner, as if nothing had happened. Every now and then, however, they'd exchange a private glance. The force of their brief intimacy would burst open inside her, quickly assuaging whatever trepidation she felt. Away from the office when she thought of him, she decided that he was a modern version of a Confucian gentleman—which struck her as archaic, but oddly charming. She did not anticipate a repeat encounter but wondered when and how he would suggest a parting of the ways (she suspected he would be generous with contacts), which might not be the worst thing. The only problem was the ferocity of their sexual encounter, which had been like nothing she'd ever known and which, when she dared to think of it, gave her pause.

Three weeks later, at the tail end of a Friday, Ted called the staff into his office and announced that Millicent would no longer work at *Worldly Affairs*. In fact, she was not coming home, and had checked herself into an apartment in a managed care facility.

There was a moment's silence.

Justin said, "So can we replace the Wang?"

Ted frowned but said "As soon as possible," signed an open purchase order on the spot, and handed it to Lei-li. "You're in charge of setting up the new system, with Justin's assistance."

They talked a little longer about the new order of things and then, at five, Ted asked Lei-li to stay for a few minutes, adding, "if you don't have a previous engagement, or date, that is? I know it's Friday."

As he closed the door, he overheard Brandon ask Justin, "What do you suppose?"

Lei-li sat awkwardly in front of his desk, thinking, here it was. The outer door slammed and she knew the boys were gone. It was the first time she had been alone with him since that night. "Ted I..."

"Please," he raised a hand. "May I offer you a wine?"

She hesitated. What she'd been thinking to tell him for days was that she might want to return to Shanghai, once he'd found a replacement for her, of course. Instead, her boss was holding out a glass to her, seductive with its crystal sparkle, with its promise of something difficult to define, but larger perhaps than even Shanghai.

Lei-li accepted the red wine. "How is Miss Parsons?"

"It's sweet of you to ask." He took a long swallow. "The truth is, she's not doing terribly well at all. The operation was hard on her."

"She's not young."

"I know."

He looked so sorrowful that Lei-li was alarmed for a moment.

"You're young," Ted said, and then with a glint Lei-li would later think of as his most seductive quality, added, "too young for me?"

She blushed violently and quickly drank some wine to cover her embarrassment.

"Do you have something to do tonight?" he asked.

"Just some reading."

Her answer was at once reassuring and provocative. "Tell me about yourself," he said, as he glanced around, his eyes searching for something. Lei-li picked up his cigarettes, which were sitting on his desk by the globe, where he always seemed to leave them.

She held them up and helped herself to one. "Yes?"

He smiled. "It's just you and me now, kiddo, isn't it?"

Afterwards, when she left, Ted saw that two hours had slid by in easy conversation. He was wrong about her. She was less comfortable in this country than he originally thought, and terribly homesick for Shanghai. Shyer, too, than he expected, and he refrained from kissing her, although he wanted to. He had taken her hand instead, caressed it, and she had hesitated at first but not pulled away, which he took as a good sign. Not too young for him though, *hardly*. Millicent had hinted as much.

The stripper had been fifteen or so years his senior, not much older than Lei-li was now. When she told him she intended to keep the baby he had at first gone to Millicent to say he ought to do the right thing, marry her and raise their child. It had been a late fall afternoon, much like today, and his cousin poured him a glass of sherry. And then, she proceeded to tell him all about *Worldly Affairs*, that she would have no one to give this to, and if he would do it, she would solve his present problem. "Later," she had said. "You don't have to come on board with me now—finish college, go do your own thing first—but promise you'll come back later when I need someone. There's time. It's a life; you'll see."

Light faded; evening settled in. Shanghai, Lei-li said, had excellent gourmet restaurants, and every week, there was some major international conference taking place. Ted knew the flight would be unbearably long, but no worse than to Australia or South Africa. Her eyes lit up when he said that some folks at Yale were planning a conference in China next year and wanted them there. The possibilities, he told her, were endless if she chose to stay. *With me,* he almost said, but stopped himself. He didn't want to scare her off. He could be patient when needed. This wasn't only about sex, hardly, but Ted felt a certainty about her that was unexpected and strangely pleasurable.

He closed up the office. Interesting how firmly Lei-li declined his dinner invitation tonight at Sasha's. He liked her independence and reserve. Earlier that day, Millicent had declared, almost gleefully he thought, that it was now time at last for her to retire, done as she was with *Worldly Affairs.* Ted did not argue because, well, because *when* had he ever, really? Before he went the way of Millicent, dozens of Ashleys, Brandons, and Justins would grace these premises, but if he played this hand right, only one Lei-li. He thought of the future. He thought of her breasts. He thought of Shanghai—what did they call the riverside again, the Bund? He thought of the Wang and how, one day soon, it would tumble down the slope of a waste pit and into the graveyard of history.

CIRCULAR TALES

SPACE

THE morning my nephew Francis wants to invite me to dinner, I am engrossed in an email exchange. Joshua Kaminsky is a seventy-year-old self-taught Sinologist from Berlin, now resident in New York, who has visited Shanghai. He found me in cyberspace half a year ago while researching pre-1949 Chinese hair-styles, and we've been corresponding ever since. In real time, since we both frequently cannot sleep when we ought, we sometimes "talk" for hours.

When I finally sign off, my voicemail beeps, impatient.

Francis says when I call, "Auntie Kar-Li, are you okay? Your phone was busy for so long I thought something was wrong." His voice is harrowed by concern, no doubt because my inaccessibility inconvenienced him.

I reply, "Ah, you're back in town, are you? You must have thousands of frequent flyer miles by now." It's the end of March. He was last here in February for the new year.

"Oh no, can't be bothered. Just fly the cheapest."

"You should look into those programs. It would save you money in the long run."

"Auntie Kar-Li, I don't have time like you to spare for things like that." In the background, his wife tells him to hurry up. "But listen, there's something we'd like to talk to you about tonight."

"Is this another of your get-rich-quick schemes, Francis? What was it last trip? Time shares in Nevada? I am not interested in deserts. Too many snakes and camels."

"No, no, nothing like that. You'll like this proposal we're bringing to you from our friend Betsy. She's a scholar like your friend in New Jersey. You know, Kapinsky."

"New York, Kaminsky, and he's not exactly a scholar."

"Oh, yeah, right. Anyway, this is different. Please come to dinner."

I do not trust either of my nephews or their sister. Basically, they all want me to sell my home because the money could help finance their failing lives. Like their father, my brother Kar-Hung, they're *hopeless* at business management. Francis, the eldest, has the most ridiculously over-extended schedule of anyone I know, and lacks sufficient focus for his restaurant business. I've told him time and again that if he has no interest in it, he should do something else. Jude, the younger, is an "investment counselor" who missed all the boom cycles in the stock market in favor of bonds, and when time came for bonds, sold his. Only the niece is prudent with money. She's a moralistic prude, though, who assumes her actions are entirely selfless and noble. Like mother, like daughter.

Why can't my family be like Joshua? He wants nothing from me, just occasional solace in an email, just friendship without spatial intrusion.

The problem is, I've never happily shared space. Now that I am "mature" as Joshua says—sixty-seven this spring—my younger relatives want to move me, their spinster aunt, to America. Francis is particularly insistent, assuming charge as befits his position among the siblings. He wants me to live with him and his wife in Indiana. Francis at forty does not use email. *Inconceivable* that someone less prepared for the future than I should boss me around.

My flat in Causeway Bay overlooks the Hong Kong Yacht Club. It's a large old space, one I bought half a century ago because it was close to work. My hairdresser's salon I sold two years ago. I'm done with a lifetime of curlers and neck massages for *mahjong* afternoons society matrons. Days and evenings are mine now to surf the net and do as I please.

"You'll hurt your eyes," Francis said, the last time he blew into town. "Staring so long at the computer."

"What else should I do that costs so little? Would you rather I hit the casinos?"

"If you sold this place, you'd have more than enough money to spend in America." He glanced at the stacks of boxes and general mess.

That embarrassed me. The trouble with growing old is that you lose sight of things. I *meant* to clean up the mess months ago, but somehow, days slipped past and the stacks grew. Still, I wasn't going to let him bully me. "Let me think about it."

Francis owns three Chinese restaurants around Indianapolis and claims he has no time for cyberspace. His wife Maisie, on the other hand, regularly sends emails filled with Christian prayers, which I delete without reading. She manages operations at the restaurants and sells real estate on the side.

Since my brother's death a year ago, Francis has taken to worrying about me. Guilt, no doubt, because he and his siblings insisted on moving their widowed father to such frosty climes. Kar-Hung expired in record time, out of boredom no doubt, because in their American life, there was no place for an old man who didn't live for the church. My late sister-in-law, having found God in Kowloon, conducted her religious life regardless of my brother. Her piety raised worship to new heights; she legally named their sons Francis-Assisi and Saint-Jude, and their daughter, Lots-Wife. It's a good thing no one pays attention to legal first names, neither in Hong Kong nor Indiana.

Lately, Francis visits with an alarming frequency. I am his father's only sibling.

"The community is very lively which is why people are eager to live at Betsy's home," Maisie says as she spoons more prawns into my bowl. The "home" is a retirement facility with spacious quarters for each resident, *and very reasonably priced,* she adds. *Spacious, reasonable,* Francis echoes, as if a chorus can erase his obvious complicity.

Maisie barrels on. "They have casino evenings, afternoon teas in the garden, *tai chi* at sunrise. Oh, and sometimes, even theatre matinees after Saturday brunch. The community theatre's *so* generous. They love performing *so* much they don't even charge. Last month was *The King and I!*" She has slipped into English in her excitement and doesn't even realize.

Her chopsticks have barely touched the food in her bowl. I am fascinated by the way they hover and rise, hover and rise, in time with the passions of speech. She leans forward slightly, as if to underline the importance of her words. Francis meanwhile nods emphatically, saying "really very good performance, very fine."

I murmur in Cantonese, "Only lust could make a Siamese king dance like a *gwei.*"

Maisie and Francis speak simultaneously.

"What was that?" Maisie asks.

My nephew says, "My aunt isn't familiar with the show."

"Of course I am!" I snap in English, since he knows perfectly well what I mean. "And I don't mean the remake of that stupid movie with *ChowFaan* Fat in Hollywood." I laugh noisily at my own pun, baring a mouthful of food. Francis frowns, and discreetly clamps his mouth shut, a signal to me. I ignore him. The privilege of age is to upset *bak gwei* sensibilities, these "white ghosts" who *still* boss us around, even after the end of colonial rule. American, English—barbarians are all alike, always expecting us to behave like them to be considered "civilized." I can almost forgive his wife, even though she's Chinese, because she's lived much longer over there among the barbarians. Almost. But now even Francis, who shares my blood, is infected by this barbarous strain.

Francis tries to tell Maisie about the Chinese actor whose name sounds like *chow faan*, meaning fried rice. She nods and smiles, but it's clear the joke eludes her. For the rest of the meal, I talk with my mouth full, chomping noisily. Maisie is subdued. By the time the fruit arrives, she's given up trying to sell me a space in Betsy's home.

Later, when my nephew brings me back to my flat, he says, "You weren't very nice to my wife. She was offering you a good real estate investment."

"Real estate? You mean death estate, don't you? Francis, I'm not moving into a graveyard."

"Auntie, you misunderstand. You know you can always live with us. Maisie was only trying to help her friend raise more capital."

"She's really your friend?"

"Maisie met her at a church social about half a year ago."

"Then why are you so concerned about this stranger? She just wants a sale, and sees your old aunt as prey."

Francis hesitates, and I know there's something else on his mind. "You don't understand, Auntie. She's become our friend, and brings many groups to the restaurant because the community she manages has several Asian residents. There's no need to be rude to Maisie just because she's trying to do a little extra business."

"I wasn't rude. How was I being rude?"

"You know perfectly well. You're just like *A-Ba.*"

"Your father and I keep our customs. In Hong Kong, it is *not* rude to chew with your mouth open. It allows proper mastication."

Francis simply gazes at me without speaking, like a sad mongrel destined for the pot. How did he become this way, this boy who once defied his parents to major in philosophy before succumbing to the MBA? His silence daunts. I bustle, offer tea, but he declines, saying he's full. When he bids goodnight, he says, "you should consider a hearing aid."

That night, sleep eludes me. I am furious. For one thing, I do *not* need a hearing aid. Francis says my TV's always too loud, a sign I can't hear properly. I keep my television on constantly, which annoys him.

Around two, I get up and sign on to check for messages from Joshua. There is a reply to my last email about Confucian filial piety, about familial duty which is not duty when entwined with love and respect. *A circle idea,* I had written, *where one turns into the other. Young people dismiss Confucius because they confuse the idea of duty with the travails of kinship. Duty begins within yourself, and, unlike family responsibilities, is never a burden.*

Joshua replies, *The Communists want the same thing but they substitute the state for the individual.*

I like our exchanges. It is a luxury to wander among such thoughts, instead of courting anxiety over the shampoo supply or irritation at the manicurist who *may,* if she chooses, show up on time for a change. The energy in our words calms me. I play on the net for hours until dawn seeps over the boats in the harbor below, wooden sampans parked on the water's surface, each in their own space within the typhoon shelter, protected from the perpetual and invariably repeating cycle of storms.

"That retirement home doesn't even have broadband," I tell Maisie at brunch two days later. The brochure she left was impressive, and admittedly, the returns looked tempting. But I still don't trust their motives. "Why should I invest my money in a place run by an ignoramus?"

"Forget about it, auntie. I already have. We have a more important mission today."

Maisie is constantly on a mission. Her family emigrated when she was thirteen and she found God in Indiana. She subsequently found my nephew in college, longing for homemade *won ton* noodle soup, with which she seduced him. Maisie is the reason he ended up in the restaurant business. I must concede, though, that she always finds the best *yum cha* places, even though she's only a visitor to Hong Kong these days.

We are at a restaurant in Times Square, walking distance from my home.

"All I mean is that an investment needs to be carefully considered, and some place so backwards can't really be good potential."

"Not everyone is as clever as you, my husband's *yee ma.*" She acknowledges my elder sister's status to her late father-in-law and serves me a scallop tart. "Here, try this. It's one of their *dim sum* specialties."

Maisie is clever. She knows my penchant for new cuisine. The tart is delicious.

She continues. "I'm surprised you haven't been here. So close. You really must go out more often."

Afterwards, she walks me around the shopping mall. Times Square sells everything, even pianos. I am amazed, and a little bemused to confess that it's taken me this long to come here. I was always the first to see anything new, but this building has been around, according to Maisie, for several years. She took me by the underground path from the subway station, saying, "Even when it's raining you can walk here without getting wet."

We stop at a computer store, the object of her mission. Maisie says, "Your computer is too old a model for broadband. Would you like to look at the new ones?"

The array of hardware is overwhelming. I won't admit to her that I've never shopped for any computer equipment before. One of the young hairdressers at my salon set up the system, and he signed me up for Internet access. Around Francis, it's easy to lord my expertise, but Maisie's another story.

She is obviously at home as she chats with the salesman in Chinglish about megabytes, pixels, and USB. They might as well be speaking Uyghur.

"*Yee ma* is very modern," she tells the man behind the counter. "She knows about broadband and has email friends all over the world!"

"Brilliant," says the salesman. "Need a *mon* as well?"

He means a monitor. I nod dumbly.

Maisie commandeers. "Let me take care of everything," she says, but "everything" is surprisingly inexpensive. I pay willingly.

Back at my place, Maisie turns on the TV before I do. "You like that, right? I understand. The voices keeps you company. Francis's dad was the same."

We clear out desk clutter to make space. She sets up the hardware, calls PCCW to get broadband organized. "We'll keep your dial-up until I'm sure the new access is working. Can't leave you without Internet, right?"

Maisie spends the day helping me clean up, cheerful and Christian. She never mentions either church or the retirement home. By evening, my space looks the way it used to, neat and open. The stuff which sat in boxes since the salon sold is finally sorted, put away, or bundled for rubbish collection.

Around six thirty, she says, "Well, my husband will be hungry. Are you sure you won't join us for dinner? We're going out for Peking duck tonight with some American friends. 'Other nation' people love that, you know." Maisie never calls non-Chinese *gwei* because she considers it impolite. She prefers *oi kok*. She mentions this often.

I decline, fatigued by her energy. Youth is another nation. "Thank you for taking all this trouble."

"How can your happiness be too much trouble?" She glances around the space. "Doesn't everything look so much better?"

Yes, I agree, but think, *Realtors prefer this too.*

Tonight, we are on real time.

Joshua writes. *What do you think Confucius would have said about eighty?*

The famous analect about the ages of man ends on seventy. I respond, *He did not anticipate our era.*

Joshua replies, *No he didn't, nor a relationship like ours.* He attaches a photo of himself with a :).

The image will not download. When I tell him this, but add that once broadband is working it will, he replies, *Send one of yourself too,* but hits the wrong key, sending ;0.

I have no recent photos, nor do I intend to have one taken. Our email relationship suddenly feels too intimate. I sign off without sending a reply.

Maisie arrives the next afternoon with a gorgeous floral arrangement and a toolbox. "I noticed the bathroom tap drips, and two of your curtain rods are loose."

I savor the bouquet while she busies herself. Once a week, Kam Lee Florists used to make a bouquet for the salon. They were my supplier for years. Their shop shut six months before I sold out and all the people disappeared. No goodbye, nothing, not even from the receptionist whose nails my manicurist would sometimes do for free. I miss the flowers.

"We added an extra room, you know, with its own entrance," she says as she hammers the rods back in place. "So that guests can have more privacy. My parents like it. So would you."

Her dexterity with tools is impressive. The bathroom tap is silent for the first time in months, even with the door open. Maisie's hair and makeup may need help, *serious* help, but at least she gets on with things. Most local women are hopeless, obsessed only with appearances and fashion. Though there are times I miss the salon, it's a relief not to have to listen to all those women complain that the color's too red or the cut's not right, that what they see in their imaginary mirrors may not be reflected by the mirror they must face.

I say, "It's too cold there."

She displays her key ring with its compass and thermometer. "Look, it's barely fifty in here right now. That's," she whips out a calculator, muttering *thirty two, five, nine,* "less than ten degrees Celsius. Everyone has central heating back home. It would never be this cold indoors." She tugs her sweater more tightly around herself.

"I'm used to this. Over there, what would I do? Only get in your and Francis's way."

"Your friend in New York could come see you. Or you could go see him."

"Don't be ridiculous," I snap.

She looks at me curiously. "Why is that ridiculous? You like him, don't you?"

There has always been something disconcerting about Maisie.

She will say things that Francis never dares. When I don't respond, she drops the subject. "Anyway, your family wants to see you. Lottie's twins are big now, almost three, and you've never even met them. Besides, soon it will be hard for us to come visit. You see, I'm pregnant."

Maisie glows at me. She and Francis have tried every fertility trick, no doubt because Francis can't stand it that his younger siblings should have procreated when he hasn't. He is peevish that way, like his father. She continues, "Francis wanted to wait to tell you, just in case we lost this one too. But I have a good feeling now, and besides, I'm so excited, I can't help it."

Thirty-eight, Maisie's age, is too old for any woman to be overjoyed at the prospect of labor. But I smile and wish her well.

"So you see, Auntie, you really ought to be there to see the birth of Francis' first. We can't be like Jude and his wife, who came back here last year to have their baby girl."

Jude has always been the one among my brother's children who sticks. When he was a boy, he would come to the salon to do his homework, his excuse being that it was too crowded at home. My brother's death unsettled him the most. I am about to say this but the doorbell rings and Francis arrives.

"I've told her," Maisie says to Francis. "Auntie's going to come for the birth."

Francis says, "She is?" Then, turning to me, "You are?"

"Of course she is." Maisie is impatient. "*Yee Ma* wouldn't miss such an important event." She gestures at the space with a sweep of her hand. "Doesn't the flat look nice? See, there's the new computer we bought yesterday."

Francis suddenly looks old to me. His hair is sprinkled with more white than I remember. I must get him some of that shampoo-in color. It would help.

He says, "Auntie and I need to talk, okay?"

Maisie looks like she's about to object, but then picks up the toolbox and prepares to leave.

I say, "Oh, you can leave that here. Francis will bring it back to the hotel."

"He'll forget it," she says, and tosses him a scornful look. Smiling at me, she adds, "I'll come by again tomorrow, Auntie. Help you with the broadband."

She sails out, like a voyager headed towards broader horizons. The space is bereft of energy.

"You look tired, Francis. How's business?" What I'm really wondering is how he and Maisie can afford to take time off and fly here so often, given how much they moan about finances.

"The Cheungs from Chicago want to buy me out. I wouldn't mind, but Maisie won't sell." He rolls his neck and there is a glide of vertebrae and muscle. "She's from a restaurant family," he adds, and glances at me as if to make sure that registers.

"I know that."

"She says we need a new strategy. That we have to change the menu and décor, do some marketing. But that's all very expensive."

I say, cautiously, "All businesses have to modernize."

"You didn't."

"That's what you think!" And I proceed to tell him about all the new equipment I bought, the young hairdressers I hired who knew about gels and coloring, about the makeovers in '85 and then again in '93, when I spent enormous sums on interior designers who in turn spent even greater amounts on everything from the protective cotton robes to the lighting for the mirrors. "Do you think I would have survived if I relied on the old perm and weekly shampoo-and-set business? Young women these days, and men, want a *wild* range of hairstyles, like that electric shock look. You think it's easy running a successful salon?" I exhale loudly, exhausted by my speech. For someone who almost finished an MBA, Francis is remarkably obtuse about business.

"You sound like Maisie," he says, glumly, looking more like a cowed canine than ever.

"Can't her family help?"

"They spend all their money at the casinos."

I am about to joke, *How Chinese of them,* but something in Francis' face arrests me. It's the helplessness, the same look my brother gave me at the airport before he left Hong Kong for Indiana. A look of apology that said, *But what else can I do,* because he had submitted to depending on his children, against my advice, which was exactly what my sister-in-law would have wanted.

I decide to speak plainly. "Look, I don't want to move. Nor do I want to sell my place."

Francis gazes at me without reproach. "I know, Auntie," he says. "It's what I keep trying to tell Maisie."

In the evening, I download Joshua's photo. He is a youthful seventy. Next to him is a dour Chinese girl, about ten or eleven I estimate, whom he names his "granddaughter" Jessie. This surprises. What he'd said was that he, like me, never married. I send an email inquiry.

She's my brother's daughter's adopted child. My niece and her husband were killed in the same car crash about six months ago. So now I'm her guardian.

What about your brother and his wife?

Dead.

It turns out that his other nephews and nieces all have families and couldn't handle the responsibility, or intrusion, of another child, especially an adopted one. Joshua doesn't come right out and say it, but I guess from his terse responses that he is upset at these younger family members.

She looks Southern, I say, having run out of words for this exchange.

Fujian, he replies. *I will take her there one day so that she can see her first home.*

Later, I lie in bed and think about Joshua. I understand now why he developed such an interest in things Chinese so late in life. I picture him and Jessie, this awkward duo, this young girl who still grieves her parents' passing, whom he sometimes hears crying at night, inconsolable. I imagine my dead brother gazing at the unborn child forming in Maisie's belly, hopeful that this one will live.

At the immigration barrier, Kar-Hung had squeezed my hands and said, *Family duty has its own rewards, you know,* adding, *Thank you, my elder sister, for all your love and care over the years.* I wanted to cry out after him as he vanished behind the white screens, *Then don't leave me behind!* But it was too late by then to backtrack on our disparate lives.

True to her word, Maisie returns the next day to check up on my broadband access. She has tamed her frizz of hair into a headband.

"What do you think?" she asks, pointing at her head. "Better?"

"It looks... nice," I lie.

Her lips twitch into a wrinkled smile. "Terrible, huh? *Yee Ma* always looks so well groomed I'm embarrassed to be around you."

Her blunt admission takes me aback.

She continues, "So did you manage to download the picture?"

Flustered, I show her the photo and then we have a long conversation about Jessie and Joshua. Talking to Maisie relaxes me. She is disconcerting, but she's also strangely soothing, even though I know full well the true reason she's buttering me up. Joshua recently said, *Independence does get lonesome.*

Maisie says, "Your friend looks like a honest man, and also very kind."

He is kind, and magnanimous. "I wish I had known him sooner," I say, and then, embarrassed by my admission, add, "but of course, we're very different."

"It's never too late to do something new, like make a friend. Never. Differences don't matter. God created us all the same."

We are both standing in front of the computer. I turn to Maisie to say something and catch her staring at me. The despair in her eyes! She turns her head quickly away.

"Francis told me," she says.

"What?"

"You wo... you can't help us," and then adds quickly, "It's okay. I understand. You need your space."

Her voice quivers—her god has let her down and she must now yield to the way things are, the way I am. I should be thankful, yet somehow, I feel something is missing. I would have understood impatience, even anger, but not this, not this despair.

Then, she becomes bright and chatty again, the same optimistic Maisie, telling me that she has an idea to talk to their friend Betsy about catering all the meals at the retirement home. "I can hire an American cook to help out," she says. "It's a good way to use the kitchen during the off hours and make some money. That way, we can finance the renovation that the restaurants badly need."

She chatters on, above the television. Her conversation lulls, and I suddenly recall that on the night of her and Francis's wedding dinner, my brother said to me out of earshot of the party, *I suppose I should be grateful. She'll take care of him,* and I was startled by this revelation—clearly, he did not think much of Maisie—because up till that moment, I truly thought he did.

When Maisie leaves in the afternoon, I find myself turning the TV volume up to the maximum, and realize that Francis was not wrong after all.

We cannot choose our family, nor can we choose what life sends us, Joshua emails. *But we can choose our friends.* He is chattier tonight, less formal and serious in tone, and I think perhaps his disclosure about Jessie has changed something between us.

I write, *I have a new perspective on my nephew's wife. She is more capable than I imagined.*

And then, I ask about Jessie's adaptation to America—she was adopted when she was five and spoke no English—and he says that youth is resilient but that his niece, who was already in her early forties at the time, was remarkable for her willingness to embrace life at every turn. *She took intensive Chinese classes before Jessie came so that*

*she could speak to her child. I feel inadequate. My Chinese is very limited,
as you know.*

I would have liked to have known his niece, I think, as would
my brother, who, among his many enterprises, taught both Mandarin
and Cantonese to foreigners. I tell Joshua this, adding, *Do you suppose
that those we knew who are now in the nation of the dead can become
acquainted?*

If we introduce them, he replies, followed by three :).

Francis and Maisie come together to see me one last time before
their return flight. I order in a substantial dinner from the most reliable
neighborhood Shanghainese place. "Little dragon-basket dumplings"
are Francis's favorite.   Xiaolongbao

"It might be awhile before we can come back," Francis says, as he
pops a whole one into his mouth. The soup bursts out of the wrapper
and leaks down his chin.

"*Aiyaa,* you're making a mess," Maisie says. "Look at him, Auntie,
just like a kid."

My nephew chews the hot, pork-filled dumpling gingerly, his
mouth wide open as he blows out air to cool it down.

I say, "He always ate too fast. His mother used to scold him all
the time."

Maisie laughs. "Didn't learn though, did he?"

"It's a good thing he has you," I say, and Maisie beams a huge
smile at me. Francis looks at me quizzically with an expression that
reminds me of my brother.

"You know," I say, "if it's too inconvenient for you to come see me,
perhaps I can go visit instead?"

My nephew and his wife glance at each other.

I continue. "I mean, I wouldn't impose on you all the time. I can
take turns, stay with your brother and sister, and even go to New
York." My words come out in a rush now, unstoppable. "Joshua's little
girl, it would be good, don't you think, if maybe I met her and help a

little? It must be hard for him since he doesn't know many Chinese people."

Francis looks ready to object, but his wife touches her hand lightly to his, and he remains silent. Maisie speaks slowly, deliberately. "I think that would be a very good thing." She spoons some noodles into my bowl. "Here, Auntie, eat before this goes cold."

I pick up my bowl, feeling faintly puzzled but nonetheless relieved. The trouble with growing old is that you cannot always believe your senses or trust that your judgments are sound. The future dances to the rhythms of youth, not age. But as Josh says, we do have a lifetime of instincts to cushion our falls. I position my chopsticks to shovel the thick, oily noodles into my mouth. Something else occurs to me. My chopsticks hover over the food as I look at Maisie and ask, "Do you think the people at your friend's retirement home might need a hairdresser?"

TO BODY TO CHICKEN

"TO *chicken*, that should be a verb," Teresa said. The teacher asked if she was thinking of chickening out, or even funky-chickening. "The dance for losers," was what he said, cackling to himself. Teresa Teng Lai-sin shook her head, not comprehending either expression. What she was mulling over at English class that day was the Cantonese verb *jouh*, which the dictionary defined as *to do*. *To do chicken*, meaning *to be a prostitute*, sounded clumsy. *To chicken*, she decided. That made more sense. She explained as best she could in her halting English.

It was already 2007 when our story began, so this was not the famous Teresa Teng, romantic singer of yore, although our heroine's mother had been an ardent fan, and thus her daughter was named. *You're joking, right?* The manager at Big Boy Massage in Tsimshatsui laughed, the first day she came to work there, not believing it was really her name. Now, everyone at work called her Teng Lai-gwan, the singer's more familiar Chinese name.

But at English class that afternoon, in an airless office above a noodle shop near her job, Teresa didn't care what her name was.

The teacher was a young Norwegian who spoke with a clipped, exact accent. "No," he said. "*To chicken* is not a verb. What you mean is *to be a chicken*." He paused, momentarily flummoxed, and added, "Although in English, that has a different meaning."

Teresa groaned. "So difficult. Need so many words to say one thing."

At work that evening, things were quiet for the first hour or so and she took the opportunity to review her lesson. If what the teacher said was true, then perhaps *to body* wasn't a verb either. *I body you*, she had wanted to say earlier, when asked to construct a sentence with a newly learned verb, but chose *chicken* instead because it was provocative, something the teacher seemed to like. *She chicken because she want to make a lot money*. The rest of the class had laughed in apparent comprehension; the teacher frowned.

"Twenty-five," the manager called Teresa's number. "Half part feet and one part body," he instructed in Cantonese. A *part*, as a session was called, fifty minutes being the unit, cost HK$225, the equivalent of US$29, a steal by many standards. The customer at the front counter was a thin blonde woman. Teresa brought her to the massage chair, where she prepared the water for a foot soak. "It's so peaceful in here," the woman said, as she leaned back into the undulating wooden rollers and dipped both feet into the basin below. "Such a nice way to end a long day of sightseeing." Teresa smiled. "I come back few minutes, okay?" "Okay," the customer said, closing her eyes.

Halfway through her full body massage, the customer raised her head. "Can I ask how you learned to do this? You're very good."

"Thank you very much," Teresa replied. Teresa knew Americans expected thanks for compliments, not that she minded since they tipped generously, but it was just odd. "I learn from Master Teacher."

"Here?"

"Yes. I am Hong Kong girl."

"You speak good English. Did you learn it at school?"

"I take English lessons now, because of job. Many foreign customers speak English."

"Mmmh," said the woman. She put her head back down and was silent for the rest of her seventy-five minutes, or one-and-a-half-part session.

In fact, Teresa had studied English at school, the way everyone else had, something she never admitted to tourists who wouldn't know anyway. Her school had been Chinese-medium, where the English teachers were not native speakers and some might even have considered *to body* quite an acceptable verb.

At each class, since she'd started these English lessons two months ago, her weekly assignment was to use a new word in a sentence. The first two weeks had been devoted to concrete nouns, and Teresa wondered whether *oil* could be considered concrete, given its liquid state. To describe what she did at work, she said *I help you push oil,* which was how the industry's language translated from Chinese, but the teacher suggested that *rub* might be a better verb to use for *oil.* After four lessons, Teresa concluded that English was nothing like in the dictionary.

But as she signed out of work that night, *I body you* echoed in her head. She had wanted to ask the teacher earlier whether or not this was correct, but he was generally so morose and stern that she felt questions were not very welcome.

Her father was up, unfortunately, when she arrived home.

"Late enough for you, hah? Young lady, one night you're going to be raped wandering around in the city like that."

"Please A-Ba. I'm tired."

"Of course you're tired! This 'night-style' work is always tiring. Lucky your mother's 'passed over life' so she doesn't have to cry in this life for you."

"Shut your mouth, can you? Just for one night? Besides, it's late. Come on, I'll take you to the bedroom."

She helped her half-blind father out of his chair and led him to his room. Her older brother was already asleep, but Teresa knew A-Ba sometimes suffered from insomnia and would stumble his way back into the living room just to annoy her. *I body you*—like the *om* of Zen—as she made sure her father was properly situated. *I body you.*

It was around five a.m. when a commotion woke her. Teresa peered out the window of their flat and saw the police leading away the woman who lived two doors down. Her brother joined her at the window. "So finally nabbed, huh? I figured they would."

"What're you on about?"

"Hey, don't you know anything? She's a chicken girl. Everybody knew. She as good as hung out a shingle."

Their father spoke from behind, making them both jump. "How dare she spoil our neighborhood!" He stumbled his way to the front door and opened it. "Chicken girl!" He yelled into the dark of the corridor. "Keep her away!" But the lift door had already closed on the arrested party.

Teresa followed her father out, and placed a hand on his shoulder to calm him. He shook it away. "Don't touch me! My own daughter is just as bad as a chicken girl!" He groped his way back into the flat, and shut the door in her face. Her brother opened it seconds later.

And what would she have done if her brother hadn't been home? On her way to work later that afternoon, Teresa pondered the question. There she had been, in just a thin nightgown out in public, and did her father even care? Her brother, her only sibling, was a security guard who worked varying shifts, often overnight. She dreaded being at home alone with A-Ba and sometimes stayed out after work at the open-all-nights until dawn, her excuse being that work ended late and she was too tired to travel the hour-long bus ride home. Her father believed she slept at quarters at work and she did not tell him otherwise. He wasn't all bad, really, but if only he weren't so unreasonably nasty when he got in his moods. He once told her that at *Dai Gor,* the Chinese name for *Big Boy* (literally, *older brother*), the *dai gors* she'd meet would all be no-good losers who would only be after her body.

I body you. I body you. The bus sped along the highway towards the terminus by the harbor.

The manager buzzed her in the back room. "Twenty-five, will you do a *gweilo?*"

"Feet or body?"

"Both."

"Do I have to? I'd really rather not."

"All the guys have customers. Look, I'll explain our rules and personally come by to check."

"Do I get extra?"

"Twenty."

One of the other girls said, "Go on, do it. If he likes you he'll leave a bigger tip. The guys always do, just like the women give the guys more also."

Teresa said okay, but when she saw the customer, she immediately regretted her decision. He was massive, like the Terminator or Hulk. Feet were fine and she had foot massaged many male customers of various nationalities, and even done a few full bodies for the Japanese and Korean men who found their way to Big Boy. This, however, was her first body for a white foreigner since she started here eight months ago.

On top of everything, he was the chatty type, and, she noticed, spoke English with a strange accent, stretching out sounds in a way she hadn't heard before, not like the English, American, or Australian customers she was now used to hearing. He didn't look European either, she didn't think.

The customer was saying. "I'm from Tennessee, do you know where that is?"

Teresa was leaning into his back, trying her best to manipulate his waist bone, which was difficult to locate. It wasn't fat, just muscle, way too much muscle. He probably worked out in the gym all the time, or took steroids, or both.

"No, I don't know where?"

"In the good ol' U.S. of A. You been there?"

"Not yet. One day I go. Your home, how to spell?"

He told her, then added. "They'd love you back home."

The manager called in English from outside the curtain. "No problem in there?"

"No problem," she replied.

"Miss," Tennessee asked. "Would you mind using a little oil?"

Dead, she thought, *I'm dead on fire.* And right after the manager had left as well, timing never being his strong suit. "Er, not allowed," she said.

The man lifted the back of the cover-up shirt all customers were required to wear for cross-gender massages. "My skin's awful dry, especially in the back." He pointed at the flaking skin around his waist. "Just a little, please."

Teresa hesitated. Normally, it was no problem if she pushed oil on a man's neck or shoulders when doing a head massage. For full body oil however, only male staff could do that for a man. He seemed decent enough, though, not a *haam saap lo*, "accidentally" trying to cop a feel. Saying "don't tell manager," she grabbed the bottle of oil and rubbed a little on his dry skin, and then quickly covered him up again. "Thank you, Miss," he said. "I'll take care of you later, promise."

He was good to his word too, she decided, when she emptied her tip box later. A crisp green fifty was in there, and she was sure it was from him. Yet on her way home aboard the bus that night, she couldn't help feeling bad. *I body. Om. I body. Om.* She did not chicken. No, she did not.

Teresa was off the next day and she took her father to *dim sum* brunch at their neighborhood tea house. An elderly couple and several women from their building were at the next table.

"Did you hear?" one of the women began. "Chicken girl made bail."

The man of the couple snorted. "Police are no good. They make the chickens themselves and let them out! Half her customers are cops, everyone knows that. The arrest was just for show."

His wife nudged his elbow. "*Wei*, shut up. No one wants to hear your dirty words."

"It doesn't matter," one of the women said. "Speaking 'white,' we all know she deserves our scorn. If she didn't own her place, a landlord would have thrown her out ages ago." Seeing Teresa and her father, the woman acknowledged them. "Uncle, I hope you weren't too disturbed the other night."

He squinted at the next table. "Ah, Mrs. Woo, isn't it? Kind of you to ask. No, my son and daughter closed the window and kept the noise out. They're good children, not like that one."

Teresa nodded and did not say anything.

The rest of the day, she took care of the laundry and grocery shopping for the week. Most days before heading out to work, she cooked dinner, which her father and brother could heat up in the microwave, but on her day off, she could eat with family. Lately, though, she found this a chore, wanting instead to study her English lessons, see friends, do anything rather than trap herself at home with him. She said so to her brother that night while the two of them cleaned up after dinner.

"I get tired, you know. Massage is hard work physically."

"Change jobs then, if it's too much."

"After all the time I spent learning the trade? No way. I like it most of the time, but I'd just like a little space for myself."

Her brother glanced at their father who was in front of the television. "He's nodded off already."

"Typical," she said.

"So go out. I'll stay with him." He handed her a bowl to dry. "You shouldn't let A-Ba get you, you know. He's just lonely. And cranky because he's arthritic," he added, grinning.

She dried the bowl and set it back in place on the kitchen shelf. "Where should I go at this hour?"

"That I can't tell you."

She took a walk in the park below of their public housing estate. The evening was cool and winter was definitely in the air. Teresa liked the cold. It was less exhausting at work than in summer. Less disgusting too, what with some of the sweaty customers who came in when the weather was hot. Big Boy was a good place to work for now, better than the previous center, which had been one step up from a chicken farm. Her brother had warned her—*It'll be rough*—when she first said she wanted to learn massage. Then, she had dreams of working at one of the fancy hotel spas or ladies salons, where the rich *tai tais* went, but she soon discovered that the ladder was a long, slow climb.

I body you. English lessons were a step up to a better position.

When Tennessee showed up the next day, asking for number twenty-five, Teresa blanched. The manager accommodated his request without asking her. When she objected he said, "It's only foot today, and he behaved, didn't he?" She acquiesced, because business was slow and turning away a customer, no matter how good her reasons, was frowned upon.

"I looked for you yesterday," Tennessee said as he dipped his feet into the basin.

Teresa set the massage chair on high and pretended to busy herself. "Right temperature?" She asked, not looking up from the tap.

"Just perfect." He leaned back.

While his feet were soaking, her colleague who had seen the customer follow her, said. "Got yourself a boyfriend?"

"Shut your mouth. You know me better than that."

"*To body* is like that. Brings out the worst in you."

"Get lost."

But as she began on his left foot, after first wrapping the right in a warm towel, a deep unease cut through her. *I body you.* The words took on new meaning, and she didn't at all like what they implied.

Tennessee asked to raise the massage couch up from its prone position. "So's I can speak to you more easily," he explained.

She knelt beside his head and adjusted the lever. He turned to watch.

"Miss, you have a name?"

"Twenty-five."

"You're not just some number." Because she hesitated, he teased. "Come on, otherwise I'll call you Fairy Girl, 'cos you're as pretty as a fairy tale."

Against her better judgment, but because he hadn't tried to touch her, she told him: "Teresa."

"Like my mother."

She was back at the foot of the couch and had begun in on his left foot. "Really?"

"Yeah." He laughed quietly. "My sisters and I, we used to call her Mother Teresa."

That made her laugh too because she understood him. "Is your mother in," she stopped, trying to remember how to say where he came from. "Ten-Nussy?"

He shook his head. "No, she died last year."

The customer was quiet for several minutes after that and Teresa wished she knew what to say. She thought of appropriate Chinese expressions—*You have a hard time passing on*—but somehow, when she tried to frame the words in English they didn't come out right. How did you express sympathy to a stranger in a foreign tongue? Teresa concentrated on her work and remained silent as well.

Finally, she said. "My mother die... had died last year too. Cancer."

Tennessee stuck his head up and looked directly at her. "Oh honey, I'm sorry. You're much too young for that. My mother, she was just old and it was time. I'm very, very sorry for your loss."

She nodded, then looked up at him and smiled. "I sorry you too."

"Thank you, Teresa."

At the end of the session, Tennessee said he was leaving in the morning and discreetly handed her a folded hundred-dollar bill. She hesitated, because it was against the rules. "Go on," he said softly, flicking it towards her. "Take it. I won't tell." She did. Later, she saw that he'd also left her another fifty, one of the old violet banknotes that were gradually being phased out.

She was already on board the bus when her brother's text message bleeped. *Got to work tonight. Someone's out sick. Sorry I couldn't let you know earlier.* Teresa flipped her cell shut. *Dead.* Her father would be in a mean mood for sure.

A-Ba was dozing in front of the television when she returned, his dinner half eaten. Teresa wrapped up the remainder and put it into the fridge. She was about to wake him, but then decided to sit a moment first, before having to listen to him carp. She was thinking how wrong she'd been about Tennessee, who really was just a nice man making polite conversation, and a very generous customer. An extra hundred! And no cut to Big Boy. Nothing her father said tonight should matter.

She glanced at his sleeping form. He looked peaceful, the way he used to when Ma would massage his legs while he dozed. A-Ba's legs tended to cramp. The heavy work at construction sites didn't help although since the accident that nearly blinded him, he'd been on disability. And a royal pain.

A-Ba shifted. A faint smile lit his lips and it looked to Teresa as if he were holding a conversation, his lips moving, then stopped, and then moving again. She gazed at his legs: roughened skin, but muscular, lean, still strong. Then, she began to massage his knee joints, tentatively at first. When he didn't awaken, she pressed harder, working her fingers around the calf muscles, pulling at them, loosening the tightness, expertly feeling for the problem spots. *Lai-sin*, she thought she heard him murmur. Her mother's name, and hers. *Beautiful spirit* was how she explained her name to the teacher at the first English class, although later, when she looked up *sin* in the dictionary, she saw it also meant *fairy*.

After about ten minutes, her father opened his eyes. "You?"

"If not me then who?" She pressed his knee joints with both hands and tapped his legs as she would a customer. "There, you're done."

He nodded, groggy, then looked around. Teresa said, "I've put away your dinner already."

"Oh." He blinked. "I'll go to bed then."

"Okay." She helped him out of his chair and led him to safety.

Before she went to her room for the night, she dusted the altar where the death photo hung. The frame was slightly askew, angling her mother's face in such a way that made her look especially kind. For a moment, she wanted to play one of Ma's old Teresa Teng tapes, just like old times, when Ma would sing along. She didn't though, since it was too late and would disturb the neighborhood. Tomorrow, perhaps.

Tennessee, flying home in the morning. Teresa brought her English workbook into the bedroom to study before sleeping. Next lesson was to use a new place name in a sentence. She thought for a bit and then wrote: *The man from Tennessee said his mother had died last year, so I say I sorry him too.*

SERVITUDE

A T one thirty, Chung put away the last of the lunch things and proceeded with his toilet. He removed his suit—one of five, one for each work day—from the wardrobe, changed into a clean shirt, dressed, and, after tying his shoelaces, selected a tie from the rack and deftly knotted it. *Windsor*, he said to his late wife, repeating the lesson learned from his employer on how to tie the *sophisticated knot of suited gentlemen*. A last check in the mirror to hold the remaining white hairs in place with a little Vaseline and he was ready. By two thirty, he was well on his way to Central, speeding past Tsimshatsui, the last stop in Kowloon before the subway crossed the harbor to the island.

Emerging from exit A, he crossed the foyer of World-Wide House onto Connaught Road. The morning's drizzle had ended and the sun was drying the pavement; he carried no umbrella. He walked the familiar five minutes west, weaving slowly through the weekday crowd, his balance steady despite his stooped shoulders. At *Henry Suen's building*—he still called it his boss's building even though Suen Enterprises no longer owned it—the security guard returned his greeting, pressed the lift button, and held the door open for him. Tenth floor to the *office that looks out to the harbor*, the one that had seen its view progressively blocked and altered over the past forty-five years, which was almost as long as Chung had been going there every single weekday, without fail, except for public holidays and the one week's vacation Henry Suen granted him each year.

When our story began, it was exactly ten years to the day that Chung had officially retired, at the age of sixty-five, a month and a day after Hong Kong was returned to China. Henry Suen did not observe such pedestrian anniversaries, because between Suen Enterprises and the large, extended Suen family, there were more birthdays (both lunar and Western calendars), weddings, funerals, newborn full-month dinners, retirements, new appointments, as well as a host of other incomprehensible occasions to celebrate and recall (his third son's daughter had presented him with a card for Grandparents Day of all things). So Suen was not thinking of his long-time bookkeeper-cum-chief-accountant's retirement anniversary, or the handover, when his employee arrived that afternoon.

"We must check the share certificates today, mustn't we, Ah Chung?" Suen said, as soon as he saw him. "You did bring the key, didn't you?"

Chung removed his suit jacket, and hung it on the coat rack—the rack he'd been instructed to purchase fifteen years earlier, when, after more than half a century's service, the original (acquired by Suen's father) broke. "Yes, I have the key, Mr. Suen. We must check right away."

"How is the market today?"

"The Hang Seng's up." In fact, the index was down, but Chung hadn't checked at the MTR station, where share prices were broad-cast all day long on suspended TV monitors. He seldom bothered anymore, although he occasionally did, *just to see, curious you know.* He had never purchased any shares in any company, despite his wife's constant urging to do so. *I just don't like gambling, never will. Only the rich afford that luxury.*

"Ahh, that's good. Come open the safe. We need to check the certificates."

Chung signaled Rayson, the personal attendant, to push Suen's wheelchair aside. The young man did and then left the room, closing the door.

"Don't like this one, Ah Chung," Suen confided as soon as the door clicked shut. "He's got a lousy temperament."

"Then you must tell Vera tomorrow. She'll do something about it," Chung responded, as he regularly had since Rayson entered the Suens' employ three years earlier. Chung liked Vera, the youngest

Suen girl—*year of the horse, always has a ready smile*—who came on Fridays. He unlatched the walnut cabinet behind the desk. The ancient safe, green paint chipping off the door, rust creeping around its black iron frame, sat on the bottom shelf, inches above ground. Crouching down, he began twirling the dial, listening for the clicks. *Right, three times, thirty-two; left, twice, fourteen; right again past zero to twenty-six and then a hard turn left to zero, and then the key... oh it's all right if I tell you.* Chung was the only other person, besides Henry Suen, who had a key. The brass skeleton with three notches: well crafted, reliable, it never failed to turn even once in all the years. *A thing of beauty.* The safe door swung open obediently.

A knock on the door interrupted.

"Go away!" Suen shouted. "We're busy."

The door opened and daughter number one, a well-dressed, self-consciously attractive middle-aged woman, stuck her head in. Chung stood up at once, guarding the open safe. *Dragon girl, the least filial. She's the one with the lousy temperament, not Rayson.*

"I don't have all afternoon, Ba," she said. "Ma wants me to remind you to be back on time today. You have to get ready for dinner at the Summer Palace?" Seeing her father's baffled expression, she added. "Shangri-La?" She made an exasperated noise. "Ah Chung, tell him."

Chung opened the desk diary and pointed to the day where he had personally inscribed the occasion. "Mr. Suen, see, you have a dinner appointment this evening at the Shangri-La Hotel restaurant. Your grandson Jaspar, number two son's middle boy, you're celebrating his exam results." And then, softer, so that the daughter wouldn't hear. "Mrs. Suen's favorite?"

Reassured, Suen smiled at his employee and then stared at his daughter. "Okay, I'll be there. Tell that—what's his name—the man on your way out."

She shook her head, impatient. "Am I your secretary? Ah Chung, you tell him," and then, as an afterthought, added, "please." On her way out, she shut the door loudly.

Suen grinned at Chung and giggled like a child. "Good thing she didn't see, huh?" He indicated the open safe.

"Yes, Mr. Suen." Chung crouched down again and removed the stack of large white envelopes, rubber-banded, each one neatly labeled in his own hand with the name and quantity of shares as well as the purchase date and price. The ink—*Pelican, that's the best*—had faded to pale violet, almost translucent. Written with *my Montblanc fountain pen, a ten-year service gift, you know,* the one clipped to his shirt pocket.

In fact, Chung was more upset at the interruption than he let on, as upset as Suen himself would have been before the onset of his Alzheimer's. *Mr. Suen hates disorder; he has a very orderly mind and is strict about observing schedules.* Chung placed the bundle on the desk and wheeled Suen back into place. *That daughter is ungrateful, and nasty. She should know better than to burst into her father's office before three forty-five. All the others observe the schedule. Why can't she? It's not too much to ask, is it? Not for a man who's dedicated his life to his family. How many times has Mr. Suen bailed out that useless playboy husband of hers for his gambling debts, huh? Lost count! Just so she can continue to show her face at the Jockey Club.*

For the next half hour, Chung placed each certificate on the desk for the old man to study—useless certificates, since all paper records had long been electronically converted. That Suen's share holdings were in reality now managed by number three son, the stockbroker, was not something Chung troubled his boss with. *Mr. Suen is a distinguished man and no longer needs to concern himself with details. He just likes me to count the certificates, to make sure they're all there. That's my job, so I do it.*

Today, however, Suen was less interested than usual. Halfway through the daily count, he abruptly released the lever on his chair and wheeled himself over to the window. "Hey Ah Chung, look." He pointed to a helicopter over the harbor. "Big bird, big bird," and clapped his hands, his eyes following the path of flight.

Chung followed him to the window and gazed down at his

employer. "Yes, Mr. Suen. It is big." *But it's sad, seeing him like this. Good thing he doesn't know.*

Minutes later, Suen looked up at his employee. "Ah Chung! What are you doing here? Go back to your work. You should know better than to be standing around, doing nothing."

"Yes, I'm sorry Mr. Suen. Right away."

By three forty-five, all the certificates were returned in good order to their place, the safe locked, and the walnut cabinet doors latched until the next afternoon.

Chung went to summon Rayson. The man switched off his PDA, on which he'd been playing the latest downloaded game, and whisked Henry Suen out of his office to the waiting chauffeur below. *Not a bad fellow, really. Polite enough, does his job okay. Could be a little friendlier, though, but young people today are all so surly. They have too much pressure, you know, not like when we were young.*

At four, Chung turned off the lights, checked that the windows were all shut—*sometimes he opens the bathroom window*—and was about to leave, when the phone rang.

It was Mrs. Suen. "Ah Chung, he's left, hah?" Before Chung could reply, she continued. "Good. Oh, you can wait till my son calls? Should be soon. He has something to tell you."

"But..." He stopped, because Mrs. Suen had already hung up, *a bad habit of hers, never even says goodbye or thank you, just hangs up on everyone all the time, even her own husband, but he got used to it and never complained.*

Should he wait, Chung wondered. If son number two—Mrs. Suen could only mean that one—needed to talk, he knew how to reach him at home. *Inconsiderate, though, just like his mother. A spoilt brat from the time he was a boy. Mr. Suen would never make such an unreasonable demand, because he respects my personal time.*

Chung glanced around for a newspaper, thinking to while away the time until the call came. The office was strangely empty, he noticed. The electric kettle Vera bought her father was missing from the shelf in the reception area. He switched the lights back on and studied the

two-room space. A small office, one that had satisfied Henry Suen for
a lifetime. Even after Suen Enterprises sold the building, and all their
former office space had been leased out by the new owners, Henry
Suen kept this one private office with its harbor view and inner reception area, where his late secretary used to sit. Chung's old office was
gone, not that he needed it any longer.

And now he saw that the goldfish etching was gone as well—
witness the leftover dark imprint—the one that had hung on the
center wall for as long as Chung could remember. When had that
been removed? He opened the door to Suen's office and realized that
the only thing remaining on the bookshelf was the framed certificate from the Stock Exchange honoring Henry Suen. *It wasn't a real
honor, just some kind of recognition award that hundreds of people get.
Vera framed it anyway, because she knows her father is the old-fashioned
kind of businessman, only understands family, not community, and he
never even finished high school so no degrees for display. How proud he
was of that, saying he'd done his duty to Hong Kong as well as his family.
How proud. Vera's always been a good girl.*

The ringing phone interrupted the conversation with his wife.
"Hey Ah Chung," said the number-two Suen son. "I've been meaning
to call you since last week but you know how busy things get."

"Last week?"

"Yes, when we agreed to surrender our lease. Didn't Rayson tell
you?"

"The lease for the office? But where will your father go?"

There was an awkward silence. Finally number-two Suen said.
"Ah Chung, the old man's gone, you know that. I mean, what with the
Alzheimer's."

"I see."

"Anyway, Ma thought it better for him to stay at home from now
on, so we returned the office to the building. They can get good rent
for it. Hey, you can only ask for a favor for so long, right, right?" He
chortled in that rough way Chung despised, had always despised.

Tongue frozen, Chung remained silent.

Suen number two said. "You still there?"

"Yes, Mr. Suen."

"So you need to remove those stupid share certificates and dispose of them."

"The share certificates?"

"Right."

"And the safe, the key?'

"The building management will junk the safe—it's a useless old thing now, hah—so you can junk the key as well. Oh, and leave the office keys inside and just single-lock the door with the handle button. The management will pick those up in the morning."

"Junk the key..."

"What's the matter, Chung, is it my cell? Can't you hear properly? Listen, I'm in a hurry, have to get going."

Chung pulled himself together and cleared his throat. "That must be it, bad reception. Very well, Mr. Suen, I'll take care of everything."

"Oh, and my brother will transfer to your account the amount..."

But he cut him short. "No need to speak of that. Whatever the Suen family wishes to do is acceptable to me, as you know."

Yet afterwards, after he'd bagged the certificates and the framed award in a plastic bag *(fortunately, not everything had been emptied out of the office)* and disposed of it in the building's rubbish room, he could not throw away the key. It seemed sacrilegious to discard the one thing Henry Suen still always recognized. When he exited Henry Suen's building, the sky was already darkening. How late was it? Chung had lost track of time and no longer wore a watch. His body knew the afternoon hours it needed to know, the way it knew the weather, and had for the past eight years, since the Suen family summoned him out of retirement into this part-time, daily role, after Henry Suen's Alzheimer's had been diagnosed. After all, Chung was a widower. His wife's unexpected death, even though she was the younger. No children, no known relatives in Hong Kong. What else should he do?

Ah Chung stepped out into the evening, his gait a little less steady than it had been earlier that day. In his pocket, the key clinked on the chain against his personal keys. Crowds surged along the pavement, headed hither and yon, to a thousand appointments and families and friends and overtime hours in ten thousand tiny office spaces. As our story ends, the workday in this year and time had pushed later into evening than Chung had ever known during his entire work life in the service of Henry Suen. Seven was the new five, nine the dinner hour in many Hong Kong homes. It was six thirty now, because he had lingered longer than he knew, reading those share certificates one by one for the last time. The city honked horns, pounded footsteps on pavements, gushed humanity into the caverns of subways and the ordered queues of surface transport.

He began the walk back to the subway exit, slowly at first, ignoring the crowds around him. His shoulders stooped—to a passerby, he might have looked tired—but it was not fatigue that troubled him. He needed something to tell her, so she wouldn't worry the way she had back when retirement ended his income. *We're not broke*, he'd reassured her, because the pension was more than generous, but she hadn't believed him then and now all he could do was keep reassuring her, keep telling her stories of all the Suens, the huge clan of Suens and their business dealings and private lives, especially Henry Suen, the man who gave him face despite his lowly role, repeating the subject that dominated their nightly conversations forever.

What could he tell her now?

He fingered the key in his pocket, caressing its familiar shape, willing it to show him what to do here, now, in this place and time before he was forced to face her, before that moment at the end of each work day, when he need no longer be merely the Suens' servant, Ah Chung. An idea formed, grew, and his gait quickened. Four and a half minutes, five, and he was on the steps of World-Wide House.

Vera, he began. *Vera Suen will call tomorrow—it's her day, after all, Friday—to tell me what my new job will be. You just wait and see. Henry Suen needs me. He always will. We won't have anything to worry about as long as Henry Suen is alive. Promise.*

FAIRY TALES

ACCESS

I T was an ordinary savings account, promising paperless Internet access. Elna opened it with her fifteen-hundred-dollar tax refund. The bank's mailer offered extraordinarily good interest rates and arrived the same day as her check. This was early in the summer, before rates slid seriously downwards and then shriveled up after the towers vanished that fall.

The bank's first piece of correspondence boomed, *ELNA, WE THANK YOU FOR YOUR BUSINESS. YOU WILL NOT BE DISAPPOINTED.* The package contained a CD-ROM disk with easy installation software. It took less than ten minutes to get up and running with a direct link to her account. There it was, $1,500 plus a $20 new account bonus, and statements she could view online. It was like this secret place only she knew of, not to be shared with Mother or anyone else.

Elna had moved "back home" since Hélene, her seventy-year-old mother, fell and suffered dizzy spells. A temporary arrangement, she assured Stan, her husband, until she could get full-time care for Mother, and besides, they only lived in the next town, twenty minutes away, so it wasn't *really* like moving out. Hélene recovered, but as time passed, a caregiver did not emerge. Elna still came home every day at noon to make lunch for Stan, who supervised the night shift at Federal Express, and sometimes in the afternoons, they made love. Now, two months since her "relocation," as the family termed it, Hélene had grown used to her daughter's presence.

When they discussed the situation a week earlier, Stan said, "We're losing the summer. Get your sister-in-law to help out. She could take a break from that stupid romance trash she's always reading."

Elna worried her facial pressure points. "I'm interviewing another woman next week. She sounds promising."

Stan craned his neck back a notch, a statement of displeasure. "Myrna's got nothing better to do except maybe pay the cleaning lady and decide which take-out to choose for dinner, assuming they aren't going out. You have a real job."

"Okay, I'll talk to her."

But they both knew she wouldn't.

Over the past year, Elna had grown her business by designing resumes. This was in addition to the clients who came to her for flyers, brochures, and other basic graphic production. *Nothing fancy*, she told people, and her customers returned because she guaranteed fast turnaround and charged reasonable rates. Her home business was a little over two years old. When her employer of ten years—a mid-size construction management firm, where she'd been the office manager—had shut down, Elna invested her unemployment towards a new life.

These days, mornings were spent cleaning Mother's home and making up meals for the day, so that all Hélene had to do was pop the tightly wrapped dishes into the microwave. Her own work she did between three thirty and ten, after Stan left for work and before Mother went to bed at eleven. Often, Hélene would summon her as early as six or seven in the morning because of some imaginary crisis. Elna's brother Matt lived two blocks away, but it never occurred to their mother to call her daughter-in-law. Myrna, Hélene insisted, was *virtually* a bride, having been married only two years, and had *way* too many social obligations that were absolutely, positively *vital* to Matt's career, and needed her beauty sleep.

The first time Elna experienced a problem using her PIN number for the account, her system crashed. She had rented a laptop so that she could keep working at Mother's. Hélene watched suspiciously as she plugged it into the phone line. Muttering something about electrical currents going haywire, she went back to flipping through TV channels. Hélene had never touched even a typewriter.

"I didn't like that one," she declared, meaning the Mexican woman who had come for an interview earlier that evening.

Elna said, "She seemed nice," but was preoccupied with rebooting the computer.

"She sounded... uneducated."

"It was just her accent." Elna knew the woman was fine, the way several others had been—on top of which, this one was legal *and* a real nurse. Once, she would have accused Mother of prejudice. Hélene's spoken English, though cultured, was equally as accented. Elna's Portuguese-American father had been a retired banker, still vital at fifty-six, when he met and married Elna's mother, a Lebanese-Chinese from France. Hélene arrived in New York in her early thirties as an "art model" and quickly discovered she wouldn't have quite the stature she had in Paris. Marriage, on the other hand, assured ease of immigration and a measure of privilege as a widow, which she'd been for the past eight years.

When Elna had brought Stan home seven years ago, she was twenty-eight and he, thirty-four.

"The night shift," her mother said afterwards. "Why on earth does he do that?"

"Freedom in daylight," she responded. They were married two years later, once she agreed not to have children, about which Stan was adamant because his own childhood had been abused. Elna hadn't cared, not really, although lately she thought Stan unduly cautious, because he seemed wholly unlikely to be an abusive father, but then, as Mother said with an indifferent shrug when first told, *que sera, who knows for sure?* Stan said Hélene wouldn't want to be a grandmother because that would force her to become an adult. Motherhood for Hélene had merely been a prolonged adolescence.

Elna logged back onto the Net, and tried, again, to view her account. After two unsuccessful attempts, the sign on screen blared ACCESS DENIED.

Tech Support was helpful but vague. "You might have entered the wrong PIN, so that might lock you out after three tries, because of security. Or, like, we've been having problems with the website, reconstruction or something. So that could be it also?"

"What should I do?"

"You could try again later, or maybe, no, wait, I think I see something."

Elna waited, wondering why she was going through the trouble since it wasn't as if she needed to do anything to her account. In fact, she felt slightly silly causing such a fuss because all she wanted was to *see* her money. She'd never banked online before.

Tech Support continued. "Looks like maybe it was this other system glitch. Well, whatever. I've reset your account and you can go back in to pick a new PIN. But log off first, restart your computer, and then try."

"Thanks." She realized that would take too long and decided to hold off for the moment. Then, remembering, "By the way, I'm supposed to get an ATM card for withdrawals and deposits. I never got one."

"Oh." Tech Support was momentarily stumped, but brightened quickly enough. "That's not our job. You'll have to call Customer Service."

Hélene was hovering in her armchair. As soon as Elna hung up, her mother began. "I don't see why we should let a complete stranger into our home."

"She'd hardly be that. Mrs. Richardson personally recommended her. Besides, you used to have cleaning ladies come in, some of whom weren't even legal aliens." This past practice concerned Matt, who preferred the IRS at a manageable distance.

"*I* wasn't always legal, remember?" Hélene's brief, semi-legal life as an art model on a tourist visa until Dad "rescued" her was family legend.

"That was years ago Mother. It wasn't like you had to work."

"I still don't see why we need her. Things are fine the way they are. Matt likes this arrangement too."

Easy for Matt to say, Elna thought, after Mother had retired for the night. Her brother was a tax attorney in the city, and his father-in-law was a senior name partner of the firm. He took fancy holidays with the beautiful and perfect Myrna—sad, he said, how Myrna couldn't have children, which *broke her heart*, so this was the *least* he could do—and managed Mother's investments, repeating often that he would take her out *as soon as* he had time, which seldom seemed to happen. He was a year older than Elna and ambitious. There were no other siblings. In the right light, Matt could have been their father's twin.

"The house next door's up for sale. Her neighbor finally passed away." Elna told Stan this a few days later, after sex.

Stan stretched his arm, which was sore from the previous night. One of his staff had been swinging a bag of express letters around and accidentally hit him. The guy already had two warnings on record and was someone Stan was trying hard *not* to fire because, as he told Elna, *a little time is all he needs, he's a good guy, basically, just a bit too much of a clown.*

Their lovemaking positions hadn't helped his arm any.

"And your mother would take over all the decorating and virtually move in. Is that what you want?"

"Well no, but..."

"Besides, we can't afford it."

She hesitated. "You know, Matt would help."

"No."

"It's not like we wouldn't pay him back."

"C'mon, you know how I feel about getting in over our heads."

"But he's got more money than he knows what to do with. Even he says so."

He flexed his arm. "Could we talk about something else?"

Secretly, Elna thought her mother managed fine on her own. To say so would disappoint Hélene, who liked being cared for. Somehow, this situation had grown out of control, and Mother had come to depend on her in a way that made Elna feel useful. It wasn't that she felt useless or anything, and she and Stan really were happy together, but something about the daily contact revived an ancient, familial sensation. It had always been Mother and Matt, with Elna trailing far behind, forgotten, until now.

That evening, she called Mother a little after six. It was a good day, because Hélene was dismissive, absorbed as she was in *Rosie the Riveter*, a movie she claimed she had never heard of or seen. Even though Mother was wrong about the movie, Elna didn't argue, happy to be freed to work. At nine thirty, she did a last check of email. Her inbox was empty. She was about to power down, but remembered she hadn't reset the PIN number.

She chose 9270, her parents' ages, reasoning that this would give her an excuse to update the PIN annually. Both their birthdays were in February, which would make remembering easy. This sign-in was smooth, and her account flashed up on-screen within seconds.

The balance read $3,020. Elna blinked. She must be reading wrong. Clicking open the activity screen, she searched for signs of an erroneous deposit. Yet the only addition she saw was the $20 bonus, which made $3,000 look like the initial deposit. Pulling up the number for Customer Service, she recalled she hadn't yet spoken to them about the ATM card.

Customer Service was friendly but firm. "Your deposit was $3,000. Are you sure you didn't make a mistake?"

"I don't think I'd make that kind of mistake." She tried to laugh, but a weak titter was all that emerged.

"Well, if it *is* an error in your favor, we'll fix it. You can bet on that! In the meantime, let's just make sure we get you that card, okay?" The Midwestern voice reassured her from somewhere in Colorado or Kansas.

That night, Elna dreamt a line of Mexican women waited at her mother's door, while Mother let one in at a time, saying of each, "I don't like her."

A week later, Elna's balance read $96,020. That amounted to more than the remaining mortgage on her and Stan's home.

She tried to tell Stan. "This account. I don't get it. It's as if my money's doubling every day."

"What account?" His arm had not improved. He was beginning to concede that it was time for the doctor.

"That Internet bank I told you about, remember? Where I deposited my tax refund?"

"You got a refund? Hey, you must be doing something right."

They filed separately since starting her business, on Matt's advice. Elna wasn't sure why this was necessary, but Stan didn't seem concerned one way or another. He began telling her about his arm, and somehow they never got back to the subject of the money.

When she tried to tell Mother, Elna never got past the notion of a bank without branches.

"It can't be a real bank," her mother said. "You must have made a mistake. How can you get your money out if there aren't any branches?"

"At an ATM."

"Those machine things? The only time I used one, it *consumed* my card. I told the manager that I wouldn't bother to use it ever again, and you know something? I never have."

"Yes, Mother."

"And you know what else? Tellers are awfully slow nowadays. You should see how long the lines are at the banks. I told Matt he had to take care of all deposits because I refuse to waste my time like that. He's *so* good about things, considering how busy he is."

Elna knew it was pointless saying anything more. She supposed it had to be some computer error which would eventually right itself. But imagine paying off their mortgage and *still* having enough to take the kind of vacation Matt and Myrna and even Mother took! Not that she believed it was going to happen, but it was fun, pretending.

Besides, she and Stan wouldn't be comfortable in too much luxury anyway.

Several days later, she and Stan had their first real fight over her "relocation." He was pissed off because it was looking a lot like they might not get to go on vacation this summer. She couldn't explain herself, no matter how hard she tried, that it didn't have anything to do with him but had everything to do with something inside her.

"I thought you married me because I wasn't like them, because you and I, we still use libraries, buy secondhand. Even read for real."

"It's not that. Mother needs me now. Things have changed."

"She can't control Matt. You're convenient."

"It's not *like* that!"

Afterwards, she could not calm down, and became doubly upset that she should have exploded at Stan, who hadn't meant anything by it, nothing at all. Stan called things the way he saw them, and at heart, she knew he was right. Mother got her way. Dad, being so much older, had been a presence, the way a grandfather might have been. But Mother loomed. Nothing Elna ever did seemed to please or displease Mother, who strove to be perpetually polite and uncomplaining. Displeasure towards her was never openly stated. What Elna *didn't* get was the praise lavished on Matt. What Elna knew was that Matt, like Mother, exhibited a kind of love, the way a big brother ought, but that probably, if she weren't around, neither of them would miss her, not terribly.

Meanwhile, her account had grown to $7,776,020. During the past four business days, her deposit had tripled daily.

The Mexican lady who came to stay quit after a fortnight. It was the most stressful two weeks of Elna's life. She was almost in tears each evening after a day spent fielding Mother's numerous calls. On the worst days, she counted as many as thirty-five, each time with some seemingly innocuous comment about the help, but just loud enough for the woman to overhear. When Elna expressed even the slightest annoyance, her mother gasped audibly, as if insulted, and hung up. On occasions, Hélene called Matt, who then called Elna, who then had to call Mother back to apologize in an endless relay.

Life was frantic and disorganized. She almost missed one deadline for a client.

"You have to relax," Stan told her after the first week.

"Easy for you to say."

"Hey, it's not so bad. At least you don't have to shuttle back and forth."

"That was preferable to this."

Stan shut up, refusing to fight. Time, he believed, was on his side.

The day before the lady quit, Elna remembered her ATM card, which *still* hadn't arrived. She logged into her account and saw that it now stood at $23,328,020. For one brief moment, her heart leapt. That amount, she suspected, topped even Matt's net worth, but then she became upset at the bank's incompetence, and then checked her annoyance because the illogic was daunting. A glitch, or virus, or *something* was responsible for this last tripling.

Customer Service apologized for the missing card and promised it would be in the mail within a week. Customer Service couldn't say why her account was so large. Laughing, *Hey, too much money isn't a problem, right?*, they promised to look into it.

Elna relocated all the next week but was firm about employing a second lady, a Filipina this time.

"You'll like her," she promised Mother.

"If you say so."

Her mother lapsed back into the silence of Elna's reinstated presence.

Matt and Myrna took Hélene away for a long weekend to Paris. A spontaneous trip. All frequent flyer mileage, Matt claimed, and his client was putting them up at this swanky hotel for *next to nothing* plus throwing in a free room although sorry, only *one* extra room, and Mother *needed* the break. Besides, they couldn't all go, meaning Elna and Stan, leaving Mother's home unattended, could they? Stan cracked up when he heard. Myrna, he said, probably *needed* to go shopping on the Champs-Élysées.

On Saturday evening, Elna viewed her account. Her balance had risen to $23,335,520, an increase of $1,500 for each of the last five business days, added, she couldn't help thinking, for each day she'd been back home with Mother. The ATM card had not arrived. Elna stared at the gargantuan sum, imagining the scholarship fund Stan would love to set up at his *alma mater*, a small state college where an anonymous alumnus maintained a fund to benefit promising students from broken homes, which was how Stan afforded his degree. Mostly, though, she thought about buying the computer she badly needed and a camper, a top-of-the-line RV, to indulge all their wildest desires.

Stan was reading in the living room.

She led her husband to the computer, wanting to share the bounty even if it wasn't real. "Look at this, will you?"

The screen was black. She jabbed the keyboard, and the monitor burst back to life but the connection was gone and the account screen had vanished. "I don't get it," she said. "It was up a minute ago."

He kissed her cheek. "You're working too hard."

Something inside her felt ready to burst, but she held herself together. There was no explaining this phenomenon, if it was even happening—which, Elna sometimes felt, wasn't the case. Perhaps this was *all* imagination, this swelling of funds she couldn't possibly own. She wondered once if her brother had found out about the account and was secretly depositing money, but dismissed that as the amount grew beyond all reasonable proportions. Besides, unless an ATM card ever showed up, she still had no access to the money.

Mother, surprisingly, liked the Filipina lady. For Elna, it was an enormous relief, and she knew she could face autumn—the beginning of both her and Stan's busy periods—that year with a renewed resilience.

Towards the end of summer, she and Stan took a long overdue vacation—two and a half weeks camping in Eastern Oregon—during which she never once called Hélene. She cleaned and cooked the fish he caught; sex under the stars was as good as it got; and Stan savored having his wife all to himself, away from normal life.

They came home the night of September 10. The next morning, the Twin Towers disappeared. Life changed, irrevocably.

Within a short time, interest rates fell further.

Ten weeks later, when the dust had cleared but not settled, Elna realized that her ATM card had never arrived. She had meant to close the account, since the bank was clearly incompetent, but lately, life prompted a perpetual forgetfulness. Logging on, she saw that the balance had stalled at $23,335,520. Her calls to Customer Service and Tech Support rang, unanswered.

The next day, Mother began her calls again, with asides about the Filipina help, all of which she strenuously denied if challenged, saying it was *wonderful* to have someone around to look after her since she *couldn't possibly manage on my own*. In the week that followed, the calls mushroomed to as many as 45 a day until the woman quit.

The morning Elna prepared to relocate, her card arrived in the mail. She drove to the nearest ATM, more curious than hopeful. The gargantuan sum stared back at her, minus $20. A message flashed across the screen:

> As you have not deposited any new funds within the first six months of opening your account, the new account bonus has been withdrawn according to the terms of our agreement. We trust you are not disappointed with our service, and will continue to bank with us. Have a nice day.

The available amounts for cash withdrawal stopped at $1,500. "Another amount" was shaded, inaccessible. Elna thought about all the access denied to her and people everywhere, how so much of it was simply beyond ordinary control. She thought of Mexican cleaning ladies and Filipino domestics, especially illegal ones, all part of that huge, unbelievable mess that was downtown Manhattan, how those victims might never get a cent of the monies donated to all the good causes. How that just was the way things were, had always been, and perhaps would always be, although Stan still nurtured hope, but that was Stan, forever believing that good could come out of everyone and everything, even this. How Matt and Myrna and Mother were oblivious despite their stated concerns, since no one they knew had died, complaining about the dust and smoke, the inconvenient traffic at the tunnel, articulating their newfound security fears and patriotism. How *all their talk* wasn't one whit of what any of this was about. How they would never understand, the way Stan could, the way *they* should but couldn't because the real war, the one, true, never-ending war, was right here and also faraway, *out of their range of vision*, and fought by those who might never, ever, in their wildest imaginings, be able to open a bank account anywhere in the real or virtual world.

Elna pressed the button for $1,500; counted the crisp, green bills; and stuck them in her wallet. A slip emerged, but the card did not eject. The machine blinked a Thank you for using this ATM back at her. For a second, she wanted to pick up the phone and complain to Customer Service about the card and missing interest, which *was* her right, as well as about this whole absurd mess.

And then, the smell of frying fish wafted by, distracting her. Elna saw the take-out next door, where the help was preparing the catch of the day. A vision of summer—her husband yanking his reel up out of the river, the large fish fighting, dangling helplessly on the hook—and Stan's laughter. *Hey, hey, what d'you know, we have dinner tonight!*

Elna walked away from the ATM, steadying her pace across the parking lot. The late autumn breeze stung her eyes, recalling the day she brought Stan home for the first time. "The night shift," her mother had repeated thoughtfully. "Well I suppose there's love in the daytime, even if it is too bright." Elna hadn't been able to tell if Mother was smiling.

Crumpling up the withdrawal slip, she tossed it in the garbage. In the wealth of privilege, truth, rather than hope, was the greatest gift.

Knowledge meant a willingness to see what was there before her eyes.
Her bank, she decided, had not disappointed her.

AGORA

WHEN Walter left, abruptly, at the end of spring, her house became larger, voided of his presence. For awhile, bits of him lingered: Walter Dean, his name on the mailbox though they were not married; a set of skis, because it did not snow in Florida; one white sock in the dryer. She did not move these bits for weeks, and the sock tumbled with her wash, drying repeatedly.

That January was too warm for the roses and they died almost as soon as they bloomed. The house seemed enormous. In fact, it was slightly less than fifty square meters, tiny compared to even her rented rooms on Key West where they'd originally met, but for a seaside village on the South Island's east coast, it was average. Walter waited over two months to call, but only because he needed his skis. She told him about the roses.

"That garden will wear you down," he said. "What do you know about balancing floral cycles, or pruning trees? Or sheep?" He snorted, and she waited for him to repeat the "more sheep than people" joke— which, she'd noticed, few New Zealanders considered funny.

"Bronwyn will teach me." She meant their next-door neighbor.

"When pigs fly out my ass. Come back, Arcy. You're miserable over there. *We* were miserable."

"Why? Because *you* couldn't keep it zipped? I told you it didn't matter about Jill. You didn't have to leave." She swatted at a large fly on her arm. The fly buzzed off in a groggy spiral and flew out the open front door. "Besides, there's the house."

"Sell it. It's already worth four times what you paid."

She waited five weeks before shipping the skis and did not answer his truculent emails. By the time they arrived, ski season was over

117

in Colorado, where he now lived and where, she knew, Jill was on holiday.

Jill lived in town, Dunedin, half an hour south, and was married, but that didn't stop her from seducing Walter. Arcy had met her first at The Cafe, where Jill needed a hostess.

Jill read her application, glanced at Arcy, and stared at the form again. "Chan." She pronounced it "Chee-an." "Your family's from here, isn't it?"

Arcy shook her head. "Not exactly. My dad was a distant cousin, but after he died, Mom took me home. I was two. Never came back." Then, in response to Jill's curious stare, she explained, "My mother's American. White."

It was the same thing she'd told Walter after they made love for the first time, about being mixed race, because he could sort of but not quite tell, although for him she added, *Mom's white trash from Georgia but you'd never know it—she married up when she found Dad, even though all he was, was this itinerant Chinese shellfish trader, no fixed abode.* What Walter wanted to know was why she hadn't been back to New Zealand, seeing as how she had dual citizenship and it being such a terrific country and all. Walter sailed. His most awesome trip to date had been crewing at the America's Cup in Auckland.

Jill said. "I've been to America once, to Colorado. Aspen's for lovers." She flashed Arcy a devilish smile. "You'll do," she continued, gazing at Arcy's slim, tight physique and butt-length hair. "The guys will like you. When can you start?"

She went home happy that day, pleased that finding work proved so easy. Also, she told Walter, there was a piano at The Cafe, which meant he could gig—if he felt like it, she was quick to add. Walter earned pocket change playing light jazz. But what he cared most about since graduating from Bowdoin was sailing and his trust fund. He would get that in full when he turned twenty-five, two years shy when they met. They were the same age, their birthdays a month apart, she the younger.

Now, Walter was a month away from the money.

Now, as February drew to a close, Arcy lay on a towel in the garden, her eyes closed against the bright evening sun. Overripe pears sat around the tree by the hedge. A bird swooped down to the neatly cropped grass, pecked at a pear and flew away. Bronwyn cast a shadow, startling her.

"Sorry," Bronwyn said, "but I called from the door."

"It's okay," she replied, but caught herself thinking that this whole country was one large marketplace, people walking in and out of each other's houses and gardens, helping themselves to the fruits from your trees, the sugar in your kitchen, the logs from your woodpile, the pot in your stash. Walter encouraged this traffic, loving what he called "the friendly Kiwi way," and sometimes they quarreled over this. Since his departure however, only Bronwyn and the gardener visited.

"Have you called in sick again?"

She shrugged. It was her night off from work, but there was no need to tell Bronwyn.

"Arachne…"

"Don't call me that. You know I hate that name."

"I think it's sweet having a mythical name. Much nicer than Bronwyn."

"Only my stupid father would come up with such a stupid name. Shit. He wasn't even Greek, though that wouldn't be a good reason either."

"You're wallowing, you know that? You can't hole up by yourself forever. Face it, Arcy, Walter's a shit. And anyway, he's gone."

She raised her voice to almost a shout. "I'm not and he's not."

A jarring pause. Then, her neighbor pointed at the hedge, which was slightly overgrown. "Needs a trimming. Hey, you wouldn't happen to have a beer, would you?"

"Help yourself."

"Want to smoke?"

"Later, Bronwyn. I'm not in the mood."

Her friend stalked off, miffed. *Good riddance*, Arcy thought, despite a slight pang of guilt. It wasn't weird to want to be alone sometimes, was it?

Later, Arcy drove into town because it was music night at The Cafe. She did not tell Bronwyn, despite the cold wrath that would undoubtedly follow, accompanied by mutterings about how selfish some people were, the ones who had all the luck. Bronwyn had no car. She also had no phone, no job and no money other than what she got off the dole, plus a drug habit: pot, hash, heroin… she wasn't fussy. But she was artistic, and since leaving art school ten years earlier, was still trying to paint. *Pretending to try,* Arcy thought, with a vehemence that startled her. That wasn't being fair. Bronwyn really did try. Given her background of abuse, that she'd made it this far meant something. Besides, Bronwyn was a friend, the only one who really cared about her and not the parties Walter threw.

She floored the gas, forcing the car up the hill. The tiny Toyota barely made eighty; the speed limit was one hundred, and a Lexus tailgated, impatient for the passing lane ahead. Metric messed with her head. Numbers were either too small or big for what she knew to be true and over a year in New Zealand was still insufficient education.

The Lexus was outside The Cafe when she arrived, hogging one and a half spaces. The trunk—*boot*—was open, revealing half a drum set. The other spaces were filled. Circling back round to George Street, she parked on the corner, thinking at least this way she was pointed in the right direction for departure. It was only ten thirty, but it was a weeknight, and the Octagon was already quiet.

The Octagon was literally that. Located in the city's center, its outer concentric ring road branched off at seven points onto various streets, George pointing north where all the best shopping was housed. The Cafe was on the southeast side of the inner ring, two storefronts south of Stuart, in what had once been an antique store. The Caf(e), its unaccented E bracketed, forced the single-syllable pronunciation: Kiwi slang. Every time she looked at the sign, Arcy still thought it silly, although Walter found it hysterically funny.

When Jill opened The Cafe last summer, it quickly became a

favorite hangout of younger travelers and the arty crowd, the only ones who would pay for American cocktails. The locals drank mostly beer and wine. *Location, location and timing.* Her mother's voice. Her mother Lucy the realtor (*successful*—what other kind was there on Key West?) had lauded Arcy's "adventuresome foreign romance" with Walter, who charmed older women like Jill.

Tonight, Nick was bartending and also the acting manager since Jill was on holiday, which she "desperately needed" (*sans* husband, as she'd made a point of saying, as if to prove her independence). Her husband bankrolled the place—which was, Arcy presumed, a tax write-off, since Jill's idea of work was to hire more staff than necessary so that she could spend her time drinking the inventory and socializing. And fucking Walter.

Nick held a shaker aloft. "Mix you one? It's on me."

"There's no buyback here. Jill would kill you if she knew."

"And you're going to tell?"

She smiled. "Make it high-end."

"You got it." He pulled the Grey Goose off the top shelf.

Watching Nick perform, Arcy wanted, for one brief moment, to give in to her fellow American. Nick was a grad student at the University of Otago and would soon be returning stateside, home to Oregon. He had the hots for her, and that would have been okay because she knew there was everything to like about this tall, lean swimmer who dimpled when he smiled, who worked for a living, who inspired her to think about finishing college. *Eighteen credits short of a BA is nothing, one semester, two at most, Florida's got good schools and you'd be in-state.* Walter never talked like Nick. The trouble was, Nick felt sorry for her because of Walter and, unlike Bronwyn, Arcy couldn't see fucking someone for sympathy.

Over by the bandstand, the musicians were setting up. Arcy zeroed in on the drummer, a woman, older, thirty-something like Bronwyn. She lifted the dirtied martini in its stemmed glass off the bar counter and headed towards the stage.

"You drive a Lexus."

The drummer stared at her. "Yeah. Why?"

"Pretty fancy."

"It's my brother's." She turned away and positioned a stool behind the drum kit.

Arcy swallowed a mouthful. "Look at me. I'm talking to you."

Without turning back, the woman said. "I'm working. Can we talk later?

"I'm talking to you *now*." Her voice rose. "You shouldn't tailgate."

At the bar, Nick looked up. "Arcy," he called.

She was standing rigid, her fingers tight around the stem. Raising the glass, she downed the rest of her drink. She tapped the drummer on the shoulder with the glass. "And you shouldn't hog two parking spaces. Fucking Kiwi driver."

The woman turned on contact. "Hey, no trouble, okay? Sorry if I offended you. I was in a hurry."

"Arcy, don't," Nick called from the bar. He rounded the counter and headed towards her. "Arcy, please don't," but he arrived too late. She flung the glass at the woman, who ducked. It arced in the air, over the drum set, shattering against the cymbals.

"Christ," said the woman. "Christ." She walked off the bandstand, pushing past Arcy, who stood immobilized.

Nick placed both hands on her shoulders. "C'mon. You can sit in the office." He looked around at the spectators who gathered, focusing on the drummer. "Show's over, folks. She just lost her father, okay?" There was a sympathetic murmur in the small crowd as he led her away.

That night she stayed at Nick's. He lived in town and said she was in no condition to drive back, even though she protested, saying it was only the one drink. "It's not the drink I'm worried about," Nick said, as he made up a bed for himself on the couch. "You need to go home. *Home*, home, I mean. Back to the U.S."

After she showered, she sat in an armchair in his T-shirt (which fell halfway down her thighs), and watched him tuck in a sheet, thinking that her mother Lucy would have seduced him by now. "This *is* home. Walter will come back eventually."

He knelt to tuck in the sheet and bent forward, his back to her. "That's bullshit and you know it."

"Why did you say that about losing my father?"

"Agora."

"Say what?"

He straightened up and turned to face her. "Marketplace, public space. Private life belongs behind closed doors, not out in the world. Out there, you live for everyone else. You live public."

"You're saying I don't know how?"

He shrugged. "I'm saying maybe you could hold back a little. I'm not just talking tonight either."

"I'm so pathetic you need to lie for me?"

"Cut the self-pity. You're too smart for that."

"I'm quitting The Cafe. Screw Jill."

"That's Walter's territory. You're too good for that crap."

"Skip the boy scout, would ya?"

"It's late, Arcy. Go to bed."

She cocked her head, shifted her butt so that the T-shirt rode further up her thighs, and gathered her long hair over one shoulder. "Alone?"

A vein in his neck pulsed. She watched, fascinated. Was this how Jill did it? How her mother did it? Provoked men into submission? It hadn't been approval for a daughter's boyfriend in Lucy's eyes when she first met Walter. *Lust*—raw, palpable—had filled the space between them, and it had frightened Arcy.

But Nick, his longing gazes at the café; Nick fighting desire now did not frighten her. She visualized Jill in the back office, door latched, lifting her too-short skirt, shoving her pussy into Walter's face while outside, Arcy carried on, pretending not to know. Living public. Her mother and Jill were the same, separated by a dozen or so years, haunting the hairdresser's, the gym, the salons and spas, their bodies perpetually available, forever young.

Nick took a deep breath. "Go to bed, Arcy. I'll see you in the morning."

She quit her job the next day via email to Jill, who called, frantic. Jill thought Arcy didn't know about her and Walter, and even had the nerve to come off all sweet and consoling when he took off. After one conversation, Arcy refused to talk to her, letting all calls roll over to voicemail. Three days later, she finally erased the six messages from Jill without listening to them, and retrieved the first of the remaining two.

It was from Lucy.

"Sweetheart, you'll never believe... anyway Mother's getting *married!* You should see the ring. Two carats! It's absolutely riveting. We're doing a very quiet ceremony, just a hundred or so of the closest... anyhooooo, April, before it gets too blistering here... there's a ticket for you at your email. Oh, we're honeymooning in Paris. *Paris!* He has an *appartement* there... *too* amazing. Bring a date darling... I can send him a ticket if he's from over there... or not, there'll be plenty of available men, you know how it is here. Anyhoooo, must run. Love you."

She listened again, not quite believing, and slumped onto her sofa wondering whether to cry or laugh. Wondering also, *what bozo honeymoons in his own appartement?* Forty-four going on twenty-four, that was Mom.

Bronwyn's knock made her jump. "Hey, why have you locked the door again? Arcy, quit wallowing. It isn't good to spend so much time alone. You'll just get depressed. Come out and play."

"Go away," Arcy shouted. "It's too early to get high."

There was a pause. Then. "Arcy, sometimes, getting high's better than losing yourself. I know. I just want to help."

Arcy remained silent. After a few minutes, gravel rasped in her driveway and the gate swung shut. She did not remember till late that evening, after spending another long, silent day indoors, about the other message.

Nick's voice, a mid-range, honeyed purr (why hadn't she noticed before how sexy he sounded?): "Hey, you okay? I'm taking off in a coupla weeks, by the way. Be nice to see you before I leave so call?"

**

The house, her "crib" as South Islanders said, was once home to an old woman who looked after children, a kind of informal day-care for the area. It was the reason, the realtor explained, that bits of toys littered the place. The last residents and former owners were a couple who—and here the realtor was vague—bought the place to fix it up for sale. They weren't from around here and stayed only a short while, she thought. The house had sat unsold for almost nine months, although the realtor did not tell them that. The garden remained immaculately cared for, which gave the property appeal.

When she and Walter had first seen the house, an unpretentious oblong box with wood siding and a single-sided slope roof, it was the garden Arcy loved. January a year ago and the roses were in bloom: blood crimson, Texas yellow, salmon, and champagne. The garden was large compared to the tiny structure, a third of an acre divided into four plots for flowers, ringed by fruit trees. A macrocarpa hedge bordered the property. The camellias were hardy, requiring little care, and returned each year along with a burst of buttercups and wild-flowers. What the realtor also said was that the old woman's son was a gardener who had kept up the place even after his mother died and the new owners moved in. He did this for free. "So the garden comes with its own personal caretaker isn't that nice?" The realtor, Walter later remarked, reminded him of Lucy with her sweet, bright smile.

"*How* much?" Lucy exclaimed when Arcy called to tell her mother that she had stumbled on this gem of a house. "You're kidding, aren't you? What's it got? A hole in the roof? Termites? A ghost?"

Arcy wasn't kidding. Her own meager savings were almost enough to pay for the house outright. "So Mom, you'll loan me the difference?"

Lucy laughed. "Sweetheart, you can *have* it. A house instead of a hope chest. What a steal."

This was *adventuresome*, Arcy told Walter. There was nothing to stay home for. Cocktail waitressing paid well in the Keys, but three years after dropping out of college and saving money, her life was going nowhere until he showed up. *So let's move here for awhile,* he said. His parents were somewhere in the south of France or Italy or Monaco he wasn't sure and he had friends in Auckland or was it Christchurch? The move had been exciting, something to talk about, and everyone in her old world was envious, asking, *So when's he going to propose?,* to which she replied, *He moved in with me when he fell in love with Key West, remember? I call the shots here.* Besides, Arcy knew, it wasn't marriage that mattered, despite what Mom said.

And the house, that was hers. He "squatted" as he laughingly told all his friends and family. The family she had yet to meet. This occasionally bothered her although she never said so. Walter seemed to have enough not to have to earn, but he seldom talked about money, and she never asked. He bought flowers, presents, booze, dinners, and occasionally, groceries and household necessities. He acquired their secondhand Toyota for cash, very cheap, and covered insurance. He even paid for their first trip to New Zealand: airfare, all the hotels, car rentals, the lot; enough to reassure Lucy that her daughter wasn't supporting a man, a fate worse than aging badly.

She moved in alone. Bronwyn was the first neighbor to stop by, and Arcy was grateful for the company. When Walter moved in three weeks later, the house suddenly burst into life, neighbors visiting, new friends from town; his sailing buddies from Auckland came to party; and then Walter met Nick, one thing led to another, and Arcy had the job with Jill.

Shortly after Walter's arrival, the gardener stopped by. The man looked older and more harried than his middle age, and had bad teeth. "Sara, the lady before, didn't care when I came to tend the garden, but well, she was... you know."

Arcy had just hung up with her mother (who nagged, yet again,

But sweetie, you <u>*can*</u> *hint about getting engaged, you know after all it* <u>*has*</u>
been, what, more than a year? A <u>*little*</u> *more commitment would be nice*),
so she only half heard him. "Sorry what?"

"No worries. That's over now, isn't it? So what say you let me come
by once a fortnight. I'll start today." He peered at the over-long grass.
"Needs attention, but I didn't want to disturb until after you'd settled."

"I suppose that's fine. But you must let me pay you."

He considered this as if it were an odd suggestion. "Wouldn't
know how much to charge."

She tried not to roll her eyes. Sometimes the most straightforward things were impossible to negotiate here.

"Could I plant some lilies for market? There's some nice disturbed
soil in that corner near the camellias that doesn't get too much sun.
Lilies don't like too much sun, you know. And I could clip the roses
as well. Those will sell."

"That's fine," she said but wondered how much he really could
make.

"Right, good as gold," and he went to get the lawn mower and
tools from his van.

Like something out of another century, Walter said, watching the
man prune the hedge. *Barter, how cool is that?* But Arcy wondered
what he meant about Sara, and later that week, when they were at
their neighbors'—sitting around in the afternoon sun with wine and
cheese, listening to cool Kiwi and Aussie pop, bands neither she nor
Walter had heard before—she brought up Sara. Everyone went quiet
for a moment, which didn't escape her notice. Then someone made a
cursory remark and the conversation returned to all the amazing places
Walter had traveled to and lived in with his family. His disgustingly
rich family, as the locals laughingly said, these locals who defended
their paradise but desperately wanted more even if they pretended
otherwise. Walter was more.

"But surely you noticed?" she asked him in bed later. "No one
would tell us about Sara."

"Maybe they didn't like her?"

"There's something going on."

"Go to sleep. You're imagining things. Everyone's really nice here."

For awhile, she forgot about it. Then, Bronwyn stumbled in one afternoon, high, and in one of her down moods. Walter was out. "You're my only friend here, y'know," she said. "The rest of the village, they've got their thumbs stuck up their asses."

And what did that say about *her*, Arcy wondered, but said nothing.

"Sara was nice to me too," Bronwyn continued.

"What was she like?"

"Quiet, like you. She'd give me a coffee or beer, not like some of these others. Hell, I've lived here longer than most everyone else but because I don't *own*, they think they're better than me."

"It's not like that..."

"It is *so* like that. You should know, being Chinese and all."

Arcy ignored the remark. Bronwyn's ignorance and melodramas could be tedious, as Walter often pointed out. She had to go to work in another hour and didn't need the agitation.

"You know," Bronwyn stood up and looked around the living room. "She offed herself here. It was sad."

It came clear then why the house had been so cheap. A suicide, the details of which pieced themselves together over time via a remark from the gardener, a comment from a neighbor, even a brusque, probably conscience-stricken murmur from the realtor when Arcy confronted her. *Here one moment gone the next no one knew why exactly.* The husband traveled; the wife, it was apparent, had left very little of her own mark on the house. Which was why the bits of toys remained in corners, on windowsills, inside closets: a history she wouldn't disturb. Bronwyn wasn't sure, but she thought Sara had lived there perhaps a month, no more than two.

Once the initial horror subsided, they decided it was still a good house. *Her ghost isn't here*, Walter declared. *She must be at peace.* Arcy concurred, even though she harbored doubts, that yes, he was right. That was what it had to be because life couldn't go on otherwise. Not life the way she wanted.

"The economy must be really depressed there," Lucy said after Arcy told her the story. "Even suicide homes sell, especially if they don't feel creepy when you walk in."

Not depressed, Arcy explained. The local economy was simply catching up to the North Island and the rest of the world. Within half a year, the city council reassessed her house for two and a half times the purchase price, and now, a little over a year later, realtors were quoting four and five times her original investment. *Timing, timing, and location.* The *Lord of the Rings* films had made their paradise getaway hot.

Until Walter changed everything.

"How long have you known about Jill?" Walter asked, sheepish, the morning he said he wanted to go home, after which Arcy finally accused him outright. She had just come in from the garden, and shreds of a recent mowing stuck to her thighs.

"Pretty much since the beginning," she gazed at her boyfriend's slightly crooked mouth, the broad shoulders, pecs like the boxer he wasn't. "Bronwyn saw you two go into the toilet stall at The Cafe."

He blanched, avoided her gaze. "That never happened! You know what Bronwyn's like. How could you believe her?"

"Whatever. Toilet, office, our car for all I know. Who gives a fuck? The point is, you did, didn't you?"

"Anyway, it's over." Then, "Why didn't you say anything?"

"What's to say? It was too obvious, the way she kept drooling over you, leaning her boobs in your face."

He winced. "Don't talk about her like that."

"Why not? You don't expect me to be *happy* about this, do you?"

"It was just sex. Didn't mean anything."

"And I was...?"

He broke her gaze and went to the front of the house, which overlooked the garden. "It's not like I'm breaking up with you. This was meant to be a long trip, temporary. The house was just part of the adventure. I didn't expect this to be home."

"Well it is for the moment, mine at least. Now what am I supposed to do?"

"Look, I'm not going to repeat myself. You can either come with me or not. I mean, it's not like we ever planned on *settling* here. Besides, we're *American,* as everyone here so likes to remind us. We're *privileged.*"

She muttered. "Maybe *you* are," but he had absented himself to the bathroom.

But even that argument was futile. When she first arrived, she had been eager to look up her father's relatives, and found one of the Chan branches who had known him slightly. It was insubstantial though, nothing to hold onto. Lucy called all that "prehistoric." The day Walter left, they were still arguing over futile, insubstantial things, the way lovers will when there is nothing more to say.

**

A fortnight came and went. Nick left and she did not see him again, although he called and they spoke for awhile. He had curbed the longing in his voice, Arcy realized, and she wondered how he managed that. She mentioned Lucy's wedding. Casually, she thought. He offered congratulations, adding, his new job wouldn't have started by then yet. His voice was mildly hopeful but Arcy didn't ask him to be her date. But she let the notion float, and somehow, she knew he knew. Before he hung up he said, *So stay in touch? You have my number.*

The weather, she told herself. That was why she didn't go out and had stopped answering the door. No other reason. She had to keep the fire going for the house to hold onto warmth since it had no insulation. Harder work without Walter.

The weather was beginning to cool, and a damp chill prevailed. Arcy noticed how many spiders seemed to appear all over the house. *There are no poisonous spiders in New Zealand,* Walter reassured at the beginning. *It's the safest country in the world.*

The first spider she observed spun its web in a corner of the kitchen ceiling. A good location, she thought, where the web's survival was assured. A large fly flew in and over the days that followed, she watched, fascinated, as the trapped creature's movements slowed, then stopped. The spider, which was surprisingly small, spun its threads around the corpse. It was beautiful, this creation of the shroud.

Then, in a rush, there were spiders everywhere, in corners as expected, but also in the most absurd locations. Seated at her dining table one morning, she felt a tickle near her thigh and saw that a spider had begun its web between the chair and the table. Another afternoon, a feathery breeze against her arm proved to be a spider attaching the start of its web between her elbow and the window. That day, Bronwyn knocked and she opened the door part ways but wouldn't let her in. Bronwyn didn't want to listen about the spiders.

One night she was awoken from sleep by the very slightest tremor in her hair, where a spider was spinning between the headboard and her head.

Meanwhile, time scurried forward towards the great day on Key West.

In her little village home, Arcy watched the spiders as time crawled towards a New Zealand autumn. One day when both the fridge and the kitchen cupboard were finally empty, she made her way to the village shop—the *dairy*—to buy food. The bright sun hurt her eyes. She ran into a neighbor, who asked *So have you heard from Walter?* When Arcy didn't reply (since she suspected the woman was being catty, not neighborly), the woman babbled on, *The closer we get to winter, the crazier Bronwyn will be*, and recalled how, last winter, someone called emergency to check Bronwyn into the hospital for a few days when she'd gone off her meds. Arcy listened, nodding dumbly, and did not defend her friend, even though she knew Bronwyn had been religious about her meds for quite awhile now.

Lucy called and left cheery messages, so cheery that Arcy wondered if her mother even realized that they hadn't actually spoken for quite a time.

Nick called and left a voicemail to say he was coming back in

August, that he missed New Zealand more than he expected he would. He said he thought about her often, perhaps too often. He said she could count on him if she wanted, that there would be time.

March came and went. There was the morning Arcy shouted, really loud, *agora, agora, agora,* and then stayed in bed all day.

Bronwyn no longer came by.

Meanwhile, the spiders continued their nesting dance.

By early April, Lucy's phone messages became more frequent. At first, she asked about Arcy's dress for the wedding, but these soon gave way to insistent requests to call her back. Each time the phone rang, Arcy watched the message light blink. And each time, like a chant, she repeated, *agora.* The sound of the word, uttered into the silence and spiders, steadied her. *Agora.* It wasn't yet time.

In mid April, a policewoman knocked on her door. Arcy opened it a crack. "It's your mother, Miss," the officer said. "She's called the American embassy to track you down to see if you're all right."

"I'm fine," Arcy said. She waited a beat, so as not to act as rudely as she felt, then shut the door. A few minutes later, she heard the police car drive away.

A week before the wedding, her mother's message asked. *Do you want me to postpone the wedding, sweetheart?*

Arcy switched off the phone machine. Less than an hour earlier, she had tried to recall Walter's face, but Nick's voice had intervened.

It was time.

She unlatched the door and stepped out. The garden was verdant but the blooms were gone and the trees were showing signs of death. Right on schedule for the season. Arcy pictured her mother's wedding and the floral splendor that would grace it. It would be a grand affair. Her mother would like Nick. For an instant, she panicked, unsure of this current of thought, insular and untested. She retreated back to the house.

The front door was ajar. A spider's web hung, fully spun, between the lock and the doorjamb. A tiny spider, its web measured a mere eight centimeters—*slightly less than three inches*—in diameter. It was octagonal, or so it appeared to her naked eye but Arcy couldn't be sure. She glanced back at the garden, and the lush splendor reassured her. *Agora.* That was it. That was what had to be.

FAMINE

I escape. I board Northwest 18 to New York, via Tokyo. The engine starts; there's no going back. Yesterday, I taught the last English class and left my job of thirty-two years. Five weeks earlier, *A-Ma* died of heartbreak, within days of my father's sudden death. He was ninety-five, she ninety. Unlike *A-Ba*, who saw the world by crewing on tankers, neither my mother nor I have ever left Hong Kong.

Their deaths rid me of responsibility at last, and I could forfeit my pension and that dreary existence. I am fifty-one and an only child, unmarried.

I never expected my parents to take so long to die.

This meal is *luxurious,* better than anything I imagined.

My colleagues who fly every summer complain of the indignities of travel. Cardboard food, cramped seats, and these days, too much security. They fly Cathay, our "national" carrier. We've never been a nation; *national* isn't our adjective. *Semantics,* they say, dismissive, just as they dismiss what I say of debt, that it is not inevitable, or that children exist to be taught, not spoilt. My colleagues live in overpriced, mortgaged flats and indulge 1 to 2.5 children. Most of my students are uneducable.

Back, though, to this in-flight meal. Smoked salmon and cold shrimp, endive salad, melon to clean the palate. Then, steak with mushrooms, potatoes *au gratin,* a choice between Shiraz or Cabernet. Three cheeses, white chocolate mousse, coffee and a liqueur or brandy. Foods from the pages of a novel, perhaps.

My parents ate sparingly, long after we were no longer impoverished, and disdained "unhealthy" Western diets. *A-Ba* often said that the only thing he discovered from travel was that the world was hungry, and that there would never be enough food for everyone. It was why he did not miss the travel when he retired.

I have no complaints of my travels so far.

My complaining colleagues do not fly business. This seat is an *island* of a bed, surrounded by air. I did not mean to fly in dignity, but having never traveled in summer, or at all, I didn't plan months ahead, long before flights filled up. I simply rang the airlines and booked Northwest, the first one that had a seat, only in business class.

Friends and former students, who do fly business when their companies foot the bill, were horrified. *You paid full fare? No one does!* I have money, I replied. Why shouldn't I? *But you've given up your "rice bowl." Think of the future.*

I hate rice, even though I never left a single grain, because under my father's watchful glare, *A-Ma* inspected my bowl. Every meal, even after her eyes dimmed.

The Plaza Suite is nine hundred square feet, over three times the size of home. I wanted the Vanderbilt or Ambassador and would have settled for the Louis XV, but they were all booked. Anyway, this will have to do. *Nothing unimportant happens here at the Plaza,* is what their website literature claims.

The porter arrives, and wheels my bags in on a trolley.

My father bought our tiny flat in a village in Shatin with his disability settlement. When he was forty-five and I, one, a falling crane crushed his left leg and groin, thus ending his sailing and procreating career. Shatin isn't very rural anymore, but our home has denied progress its due. We didn't get a phone till I was in my thirties.

I tip the porter five dollars and begin unpacking the leather luggage set. There is too much space for my things.

Right about now, you're probably wondering, along with my colleagues, friends, and former students, *What on earth does she think she's doing.* It was what my parents shouted when I was twelve and went on my first hunger strike.

My parents were illiterate, both refugees from China's rural poverty. *A-Ma* fried tofu at Shatin Market. Once *A-Ba* recovered from his accident, he worked there as a cleaner, cursing his fate. They expected me to support them as soon as possible, which should have been after six years of primary school, the only compulsory education required by law in the Sixties.

As you see, I clearly had no choice but to strike, since my exam results proved I was smart enough for secondary school. My father beat me, threatened to starve me. How dare I, when others were genuinely hungry, unlike me, the only child of a tofu seller who always ate. Did I want him and *A-Ma* to die of hunger just to send me to school? How dare I risk their longevity and old age?

But I was unpacking a Spanish leather suitcase when the past, that country bumpkin's territory, so rudely interrupted.

Veronica, whom I met years ago at university, while taking a literature course, foisted this luggage on me. She's runs her family's garment enterprise, and is married to a banker. Between them and their three children, they own four flats, three cars, and at least a dozen sets of luggage. Veronica invites me out to dinner (she always pays) whenever she wants to complain about her family. Lately, we've dined often.

"Kids," she groaned over our rice porridge, two days before my trip. "My daughter won't use her brand new Loewe set because that's passé. All her friends at Stanford sling these canvas bags with one fat strap. Canvas, imagine. Not even leather."

"Ergonomics," I told her, annoyed at this bland and inexpensive meal. "It's all about weight and balance." And cost, I knew, because the young overspend to conform, just as Veronica eats rice porridge because she's overweight and no longer complains that I'm thin.

She continued. "You're welcome to take the set if you like."

"Don't worry yourself. I'll use an old school bag."

"But that's barely a cabin bag! Surely not enough to travel with."

In the end, I let her nag me into taking this set, which is more bag than clothing.

Veronica sounded worried when I left her that evening. "Are you *sure* you'll be okay?"

And would she worry, I wonder, if she could see me now, here, in this suite, this enormous space where one night's bill would have taken my parents years, no, *decades,* to earn, and even for me, four years' pay, at least when I first started teaching in my rural enclave (though you're thinking, of course, quite correctly, *what about inflation,* the thing economists cite to dismiss these longings of an English teacher who has spent her life instructing those who care not a whit for our "official language," the one they never speak, at least not if they can choose, especially not now when there is, increasingly, a choice).

My unpacking is done; the past need not intrude. I draw a bath, as one does in English Literature, to wash away the heat and grime of both cities in summer. *Why New York,* Veronica asked, at the end of our last evening together. Because, I told her, it will be like nothing I've known. For once, Veronica actually seemed to envy *me,* although perhaps it was my imagination.

The phone rings and it's Guest Relations, wishing to welcome me. The hotel must wonder, since I grace no social register. I ask for a table at Lutèce tonight. Afterwards, I tip the concierge ten dollars for successfully making the reservation. As you can see, I am no longer an ignorant bumpkin, even though I never left the schools in the New Territories, our urban countryside now that no one farms anymore. Besides, Hong Kong magazines detail lives of the rich and richer, so I've read of the famous restaurant and know about the greasy palms of New Yorkers.

I order tea and scones from Room Service. It will hold me till dinner at eight.

The first time I ever tasted tea and scones was at the home of my private student. To supplement income when I enrolled in Teacher Training, I tutored Form 5 students who needed to pass School Certificate English. This was the compromise I agreed to with my parents before they would allow me to qualify as a teacher. Oh yes, there was a second hunger strike two years prior, before they let me continue into Form 4. That time, I promised to keep working in the markets after school with *A-Ma*.

Actually, my learning English at all was a stroke of luck, since I was *hardly* at a "name school" of the elite. An American priest taught at my secondary school, so I heard a native speaker. He wasn't a very good teacher, but he paid attention to me because I was the only student who liked the subject.

Tea and scones! I am *supposed* to be eating, not dwelling on the ancient past. The opulence of the tray Room Service brings far surpasses what that pretentious woman served, mother of the hopeless boy, my first private student of many, who only passed his English exam because he cheated (he paid a friend to sit the exam for him), not that I'd ever tell, since he's now a wealthy international businessman who can hire staff to communicate in English with the rest of the world, since he still cannot, at least not with any credibility. That scone ("from Cherikoff," she bragged) was cold and dry, hard as a rock.

Hot scones, oozing with butter. *To ooze.* I like the lasciviousness of that word, with its excess of vowels, the way an excess of wealth allows people to waste kindness on me, as my former student still does, every lunar new year, by sending me a *lai see* packet with a generous check which I deposit in my parents' bank account, the way I surrender all my earnings, as any filial and responsible unmarried child should, or so they said.

I eat two scones oozing with butter and savor tea enriched by cream and sugar, here at this "greatest hotel in the world," to vanquish, once and for all, my parents' fear of death and opulence.

Eight does not come soon enough. In the taxi on the way to Lutèce, I ponder the question of pork.

When we were poor but not impoverished, *A-Ma* once dared to make pork for dinner. It was meant to be a treat, to give me a taste of meat, because I complained that tofu was bland. *A-Ba* became a vegetarian after his accident and prohibited meat at home; eunuchs are angry people. She dared because he was not eating with us that night, a rare event in our family (I think some sailors he used to know invited him out).

I shat a tapeworm the next morning—almost ten inches long—and she never cooked pork again.

I have since tasted properly cooked pork, since it's unavoidable in Chinese cuisine. In my twenties, I dined out with friends, despite my parents' objections. But friends marry and scatter; the truth is there is no one but family in the end, so over time, I submitted to their way of being and seldom took meals away from home, meals my mother cooked virtually till the day she died.

I am distracted. The real question is whether or not I should order pork tonight.

I did not expect this trip to be fraught with pork!

At Lutèce, I have the distinct impression that the two couples at the next table are talking about me. Perhaps they pity me. People often pitied me my life. *Starved of affection,* they whispered, although why they need to whisper what everyone can hear I fail to understand. All I desired was greater gastronomic variety, but my parents couldn't bear the idea of my eating without them. I endured their perpetual scrimping because they did eventually learn to leave me alone. That much filial propriety was reasonable payment. I just didn't expect them to *stop* complaining, to fear for what little fortune they had, because somewhere someone was less fortunate than they. That fear made them cling to life, forcing me to suffer their fortitude, good health, and longevity.

I should walk over to those over-dressed people and tell them how things are—about famine, I mean, the way I tried to tell my students, the way my parents dinned it into me as long as they were alive.

Famine has no menu! The waiter waits as I take too long to study the menu. He does not seem patient, making him an oxymoron in his profession. My students would no more learn the oxymoron than they would learn about famine. *Daughter, did you lecture your charges today about famine? A-Ba* asked every night before dinner. *Yes,* I learned to lie, giving him the answer he needed. This waiter could take a lesson in patience from me.

Finally, I look up at this man who twitches, and do not order pork. *Very good,* he says, as if I should be graded for my literacy in menus. He returns shortly with a bottle of the most expensive red available and now I *know* the people at the next table are staring. The minute he leaves, the taller of the two men from that table comes over.

"Excuse me, but I believe we met in March? At the U.S. Consulate cocktail in Hong Kong? You're Kwai-sin Ho, aren't you?" He extends his hand. "Peter Martin."

Insulted, it's my turn to stare at this total stranger. I look *nothing* like that simpering socialite who designs fashionable hats that are all the rage in Asia. Hats! We don't have the weather for hats, especially not those things, which are good for neither warmth nor shelter from the sun.

Besides, what use are hats for the hungry?

I do not accept his hand. "I'm her twin sister," I lie. "Kwai-sin and I are estranged."

He looks like he's about to protest, but retreats. After that, they don't stare, although I am sure they discuss me now that I've contributed gossip for those who are nurtured by the crumbs of the rich and famous.

It's my outfit, probably. Kwai-sin Ho is famous for her cheongsams, which is all she wears, the way I do. It was my idea. When we were girls together in school, I said the only thing I'd ever wear when I grew up was the cheongsam, the shapely dress with side slits and a neck-strangling collar. She grimaced and said they weren't fashionable, that only spinster schoolteachers and prostitutes wore them, which, back in the Sixties, wasn't exactly true, but Kwai-sin was neither bright nor imaginative.

That was long ago, before she became Kwai-sin in the cheongsam, once these turned fashionable again, before her father died and her mother became the mistress of a prominent businessman who whisked them into the stratosphere. For a little while, she remained my friend, but then we grew up, she married one of the shipping Lams, and became the socialite who refused, albeit politely, to recognize me the one time we bumped into each other at some function in Hong Kong.

So vengeance is mine. I will not entertain the people who fawn over her and possess no powers of recognition.

Food is getting sidelined. This is unacceptable. I cannot allow all these intrusions. I must get back to the food, which is, after all, the point of famine.

This is due to a lack of diligence, as *A-Ma* would say, this meandering from what's important, this succumbing to sloth. My mother was terrified of sloth, almost as much as she was terrified of my father.

She used to tell a legend about sloth.

There once was a man so lazy he wouldn't even lift food to his mouth. When he was young, his mother fed him, but as his mother aged, she couldn't care for him anymore. So he marries a woman who will feed him as his mother did. For a time, life is bliss.

Then one day, his wife must return to her village for her dying mother. "How will I eat?" he exclaims. The wife conjures a plan. She bakes a gigantic cookie and hangs it around his neck. All the lazy man must do is bend forward and eat. "Wonderful!" he says, and off she goes.

On the first day, the man nibbles the edge of the cookie. Each day, he nibbles further. By the fourth day, he's eaten so far down there's no more cookie unless he turns it.

However, the man's so lazy he lies down instead and waits for his wife's return. As the days pass, his stomach growls and begins to eat itself. Yet the man still won't turn the cookie. By the time his wife comes home, the lazy man has starved to death.

Memory causes such unaccountable digressions! There I was in Lutèce, noticing that people pitied me. Pity made my father livid, which he took out on *A-Ma* and me.

Perhaps people find me odd rather than pitiful. I will describe my appearance and let you judge. I am thin but not emaciated and have strong teeth. This latter feature is unusual for a Hong Kong person of my generation. Years ago, a dentist courted me. He taught me about oral hygiene, trained as he had been at an American university. Unfortunately, he was slightly rotund, which offended *A-Ba*. *A-Ma* wouldn't have minded the marriage, but she always sided with my father, who believed it wise to marry one's own physical type (illiteracy did not prevent him from developing philosophies). I was then in my mid-thirties. After the dentist, there were no other men. As a result, I never left home, which is our custom for the unmarried, a loathsome custom but difficult to overthrow. We all must pick our battles, and my acquiring English, of which my parents naturally knew not a word, was a sufficiently drastic defiance to last a lifetime, or at least till they expired.

This dinner at Lutèce has come and gone and I haven't tasted a thing. It's what happens when we converse and do not concentrate on the food. At home, we ate in the silence of *A-Ba's* rage.

A shame, but never mind, I promise to share the next bounty. This meal must have been good because the bill's in the thousands. I pay by traveler's checks because, not believing in debt, I own no credit cards.

Last night's dinner weighs, despite my excellent digestion, so I take a walk late in the afternoon and end up in Chelsea. New York streets are dirtier than I imagined. Although I did not really expect pavements of gold, in my deepest fantasies, there did reign a sheen.

The air is fetid with the day's leftover heat and odors. Under a humid, darkening sky, I almost trip over a body on the corner of Twenty-fourth and Seventh. It cannot be a corpse! Surely cadavers aren't left to rot in the streets.

A-Ma used to tell of a childhood occurrence in her village. An itinerant had stolen food from the local pig trough. The villagers caught him, beat him senseless, cut off his tongue and arms, and left him to bleed to death behind the rubbish heap. In the morning, my mother was at play, and while running, tripped over the body. She fell into a blood pool beside him. The corpse's eyes were open.

He surely didn't mean to steal, she always said, her eyes burning from the memory. *Try to forget,* my father would say. My parents specialized in memory. They both remained lucid and clear-headed till they died.

But this body moves. It's a man awakening from sleep. He mumbles. Startled, I move away. I think he's saying he's hungry.

I escape. A taxi whisks me back to my hotel, where my table is reserved at the restaurant.

The ceiling at the Oak Room is roughly four times the height of an average basketball player. The ambience is not as seductive as promised by the literature. The problem with reading the wrong kind of literature is that you are bound to be disappointed.

This is a man's restaurant, with a menu of many steaks. Hemingway and Fitzgerald used to eat here. Few of my students have heard of these two and none of them will have read their books.

As an English teacher, especially one who was not employed at a "name school" of the elite, I became increasingly marginal. Colleagues and friends converse in Cantonese, the only official language out of our three that people live as well as speak. The last time any student read an entire novel was well over twenty years ago. English Literature is not on anyone's exam roster; to desire it in a Chinese colony is as irresponsible as it was of me to master it in our former British one.

Teaching English is little else than a linguistic requirement. Once, it was my passion and flight from home. Now it's merely my entrée to this former men's club.

But I must stop thinking about literature.

The entrees make my head spin, so I turn to desserts. There's no gooseberry tart! Ever since *David Copperfield*, I've wanted to taste one (or perhaps it was another book, I don't remember). I tell the boy with the water jug this.

He says. "The magician, madam?"

"The orphan," I reply.

He stands, open-mouthed, without pouring water.

The waiter appears. "Can I help with the menu?"

"Why?" I snap. "It isn't heavy."

But what upsets me is the memory of my mother's story, which I'd long forgotten until today, just as I hoped to forget about teaching English Literature, about the uselessness of the life I prepared so hard for.

The waiter hovers. "Are you feeling okay?"

I look up at the sound of his voice and realize my hands are shaking. Calming myself, I say, "*Au jus.* The prime rib, please, and escargots to start," and on and on I go, ordering in the manner of a man who retreats to segregation, who indulges in oblivion, who shuts out the stirrings of the groin and the heart.

I wake to a ringing phone. Housekeeping wonders if they may clean. It's past noon. This must be jet lag. I tell Housekeeping, *later*.

It's so *comfortable* here I believe it's possible to forget.

I order brunch from Room Service. Five-star hotels in Hong Kong serve brunch buffets on weekends. The first time I went to one, Veronica paid. We were both students at university. The array of food made my mouth water. *Pace yourself,* Veronica said. *It's all you can eat.* I wanted to try everything, but gluttony frightened me.

Meanwhile, *A-Ba. After four or more days without food, your stomach begins to eat itself,* and his laugh, dry and caustic.

But I was choosing brunch.

Mimosa. Smoked salmon. Omelet with cheese and chives. And salad, the expensive kind that's imported back home. Room Service asks what I'd like for dessert so I say chocolate ice cream sundae. Perhaps I'm more of a bumpkin than I admit. Colleagues, friends, and former students would consider my choices boring, unsophisticated, lacking in culinary imagination. They're right, since everything I've eaten since arriving I could just as easily have obtained back home. They can't understand though. It's not *what* but *how much.*

How opulent. The opulence is what counts to stop the cannibalism of internal organs.

Will that be all?

I am tempted to say, bring me an endless buffet, whatever your chef concocts, whatever your tongues desire.

How long till my money runs out, ending this sweet exile?

Guest Relations knocks, insistent. I've not let anyone in for three days. I open the door wide to show the manager that everything's fine, that their room is not wrecked, that I am not crazy even if I'm not on the social register. It's necessary to allay fears. So I do, because I do not wish to give the wrong impression. I am not a diva or an excessively famous person who trashes hotel rooms because she can.

I say, politely, that I've been unwell, nothing serious, and to please have Housekeeping stop in. The "please" is significant; it shows I am not odd; that I am, in fact, cognizant of civilized discourse in English. The manager withdraws, relieved.

For dinner tonight, I decide on two dozen oysters, lobster, and filet mignon. I select a champagne and the wines, a white and red. Then, it occurs to me that since this is a suite, I can order enough food for a party, so I say there will be a dozen guests for dinner, possibly more. *Very good,* he says, and asks how many extra bottles of champagne and wine, to which I reply, *as many as needed.*

My students will be my guests. You mustn't think I was always disillusioned about teaching. To prove it to you I'll invite all my colleagues, a few friends, like Veronica and the dentist and even Kwai-sin and my parents. I bear no grudges; I'm not bitter. What I'm uncertain of is whether or not they will come to my supper.

This room, this endless meal can save me. I feel it. I am vanquishing my fear of death and opulence.

There was a time we did not care about opulence and dared to speak of death. You spoke of famine because everyone knew the stories from China were true. Now, everywhere, people more or less know. You could educate students about starvation in China or Africa or India because they knew it to be true, because they saw the hunger around them, among the beggars in our streets, and for some, even in their own homes. There was a time it was better *not* to have space, or things to put in that space, and to dream instead, because no one had much, except royalty and movie stars, and they were *meant* to be fantasy, somewhere in a dream of manna and celluloid.

But you can't speak of famine anymore. Anorexia's fashionable and profitable on runways so students simply *can't see the hunger.* Colleagues and friends also can't and won't speak of it, changing the subject to what they prefer to see. Even our journalists can't seem to see, preferring the reality they fashion rather than the reality that is. I get angry, but then, when I'm calm, I am simply baffled. Perhaps my parents, and friends and colleagues and memory are right, that I *am* too stubborn, perhaps even slothful because I've hidden in my parents' home, in my life as a teacher, even though the years were dreary and long, when what I truly wanted, what I desired, was to embrace the opulence, forsake the hunger, but was too lazy to turn the cookie instead.

I mustn't be angry at them, by which I mean all the *them*s, the big impersonal *they*. Like a good English teacher I say, you *must* define the *they*. Students are students and continue to make the same mistakes and all I can do is remind them that *they* are you and to please, please, try to remember because language is a root of life.

Most of the people can't be wrong all the time. Furthermore, what you can't, or won't see, *doesn't* exist.

Comfort, like food, exists, *surrounds* me here.

Not wishing to let anger get the better of me, I eat. Like the Romans, I disgorge and continue. It takes hours: three lobsters and three steaks, five glasses of champagne and six of wine; yet still the food is not enough.

The guests arrive and more keep coming. Who would have thought all these people would show up, all these people I left behind? Where do they come from? My students, colleagues, the dentist, a horde of strangers. Even Kwai-sin and her hats, and do you know, we *do* look a little alike, so Peter Martin wasn't completely wrong. I changed my language to change my life but still the past throngs, bringing all these people and their Cantonese chatter. The food is not enough; the food is never enough.

Room Service obliges round the clock.

Veronica arrives and I feel relief, because the truth is, I no longer cared for her when all we ate was rice porridge. I was ungrateful, forgetting that once she fed me my first buffet, teasing my appetite. *Come out, travel,* she urged over the years. It's not her fault I stayed at home, afraid to abandon my responsibility, traveling only in my mind.

Finally, my parents arrive. My father sits down first to the feast. His leg is whole and sperm gushes out from between his legs. *It's not so bad here,* he says, and gestures for my mother to join him. This is good. *A-Ma* will eat if *A-Ba* does, they're like that, those two. My friends don't understand, not even Veronica. She repeats what she often said, that my parents are "controlling." Perhaps, but that's unimportant. I'm only interested in not being responsible anymore.

The noise in the room is deafening. We can barely hear each other above the din. Cantonese is noisy, unlike Mandarin or English, but it is alive. This suite that was too empty is stuffed with people, all needing to be fed.

I gaze at the platters of food. What does it matter if there *are* too many mouths to feed? A phone call is all it takes to get more food, and more. I am fifty-one and have waited too long to eat. If I give in, if I let go, I will vanquish my fears. *This* is bliss, truly.

A-Ma smiles at the vast quantities of food. This pleases me because she so rarely smiles. She says, *Not like lazy cookie man, hah?*

Feeling benevolent, I smile back. *No, not like him,* I say. *Now, eat.*

OLD WIVES' TALES

TRASHY DESIRES OF WOMEN NEARING FIFTY

J ANE, *decolleté,* arrives late, as usual, for Anna's birthday dinner at the new restaurant on West Fourteenth, the one they'd been meaning to try.

"My art director wouldn't shut up," she apologizes, kissing Anna. She hands her the wrapped gift. "From both of us," and then mimes a kiss to Lily, her glance briefly troubled by the presence of David, Lily's man. "Didn't expect to see you," she says, thinking, *But we said no men.*

Lily beams. "He insisted. Besides, it's not the fiftieth." She squeezes his arm; David pretends a grimace. "Sit. Have a wine." She pours the Cabernet into the glass at the last place setting.

Anna exclaims. "You wore the dress!"

Jane sits down quickly, embarrassed. "And do you *think* he noticed?"

David smiles. "*I* noticed. It flatters you. You should show cleavage more often."

"Oh, you don't count," Jane retorts, but she blushes, pleased.

Lily glances admiringly at Jane and grins at David. "As usual, when he's right, he's right. Even if he doesn't count."

He retreats, mock-piqued, back into the half-life of the male, heterosexual fashion designer who is never uncomfortable around women, especially not these three, and opens the menu between himself and Lily. "So what are we eating tonight?"

They have grown too used to David, Jane thinks, head bent over her menu. Frank, her husband, would never insist on coming along, just as he didn't notice the new dress. Since she hasn't worn a dress in at least ten years, which is longer than they've been married, but

only by a year, it is extraordinarily obtuse, even for him. Jane's white
satin wedding pants and elongated tuxedo tails that swept the ground
behind her are legend among the girls.

Lily and David confer (*If you get the tuna I'll get the veal, deal?*) and
giggle. Even after six years, they behave like newlyweds—which, Jane
believes, has everything to do with their *not* marrying. She and Anna
exchange grins, but Jane feels the insincerity of her own. Jealous? Not
that they lust after him. *Not David, for god's sake.* Skinny, even bony,
he wears clothes too well, in contrast to Lily, who works the graveyard
shift as a printing operator to support her "habit." Lily, whose latest
sonnet collection has won her invitations to conferences in Bermuda
and Singapore. Lily, still true to her original obsession from when
they all first arrived and met in Manhattan, starry-eyed and slenderer.
The waitress—young, navel-pierced, and provocative—whips through
their food orders. Lily watches her departing form. "A butt to die for,"
she sighs.

Anna's eyes narrow. "What *will* it be like to sag into a G-string,
I wonder?"

Lily raises her wine in a toast. "Don't be bitchy on your birthday.
It's bad luck. Besides, you should talk, Miss Chinatown herself."

"Yes, but modesty forbade the baring of that much butt back
then," Anna says. "Or bust, not that I had—or have—any, unlike *some*
people." She glances at Jane. "You just have to bounce in his face, is
all."

Lily's laughter riffs through the air, infectious.

Anna is just being Anna, but Jane is slightly piqued, the way she
always is by the woman's blatant, pragmatic approach to life (*probably cultural*, Frank would say, shrugging it off, but she's not so sure).
Anna Banana from San Francisco who came east to escape being just
another banana. *Back in the Eighties, there weren't as many Asian chicks
around, and a beauty queen? Well, she was a bit irresistible,* Frank had
said after Jane agreed to marry him and he came clean about the
women he'd slept with. Anna had been a friendly fling, *just one of her
many, she probably barely remembers, we were never an item,* as Jane

and he hadn't gotten together till years later. It hadn't bothered Jane at the time, since Anna probably *had* forgotten. She didn't recognize Frank when Jane first introduced him to the girls, and even after the *oh yeah, sure,* Jane was never certain Anna really remembered. So why now does she feel this nagging threat from Anna, from both these still-unmarried "girls"?

Jane joins in the toast, feeling more exposed than she has all day in this dress.

Steak was a bad choice, Jane thinks as she walks east across town, flushed from too much wine. David was unusually entertaining tonight and she wishes now she hadn't been so snappish. Lily was right, it wasn't the fiftieth, the birthday year the three of them had pledged to celebrate together at some hedonist paradise, without their men, in order that they might lust with impunity. This year is only forty-nine.

Tonight is cooler than it has been for days, days during which Jane longs for air conditioning, even going into work early just for relief, which is unlike her. She and Frank both prefer to do without unless the heat is truly unbearable. But since menopause—three years ago hers began, she was the first, ironic for the youngest of the girls (but only by a month and a half, Anna being second-youngest)—she is never *not* hot. She of all people, Cucumber Jane herself.

Life passes her by in the form of a young and extraordinarily sexy guy, probably gay, and her head turns. When did the balance tilt so heavily in favor of youth? She remembers her mother, the classic, post-Depression housewife, aging without complaint, as if frozen like June Cleaver into the perpetual joy of Nickelodeon, at least in Pop's eyes. Pop never seemed to notice that her mother had grown fat, white-haired, and wrinkled. She was always his "beautiful girl." The two of them probably spooned right up till the moment death came to call. She imagines them entertaining the Grim Reaper; Pop saying, *Here, take a load off, put that scythe down a sec;* Mom insisting, *The pie's fresh, have a piece, or would you prefer ice cream?* Death would have been flummoxed, no match for those two, cheerful in their dotage even when Jason, her oldest sibling (twelve years her senior, four in between, she being the baby) and his wife relocated them to the old-folks home that Jane found so painful to visit. Mom had expired first; Pop followed within twenty-four hours. It's been three years but in dreams, Jane still sees them kissing in the moonlight, without the ravages of age, and sometimes, this lingering image still makes her cry.

Jane designs PowerPoint presentations for an insurance company; Frank is a contractor who specializes in offices. They both paint, although their palettes are presently caked and very dry. Art school is personal mythology, not history. Her one consolation is that she is still in the East Village, albeit now in one of the new pieces of real estate that erupted with gentrification. The other two fled uptown long ago, although in Lily's case, it was less like flight and more a chariot to Eden. Anna, typically, calling a spade a spade, said Lily hit pay dirt, but Jane suspected envy, not unlike Anna calling art school *the intellectual excuse to get your rocks off, because how different is ogling nude models from ogling dancers in strip clubs?* They often converge in Chelsea because all three work downtown, further west than east.

When she arrives home, Frank is standing by the open refrigerator. He pops a beer. On television, *The Man Show* is ending.

He kisses her, just missing her lips. "How was dinner?" His eyes never leave the screen, where the young and nubile bounce on trampolines, their legs and butts flashing, their boobs jiggling with abandon.

His stubble is rough and she rubs her cheek. "Okay," she says to his back. "I ate too much."

"You always do with your girls. Wait till it's your birthday next month. Then, you'll *really* pig out."

"Don't be gross."

"Hey, it's time for *The Daily Show*."

The fanfare of the rising globe blasts. Jane stands by the couch, where Frank has already ensconced himself. He will doze off by eleven fifteen, halfway through the satiric news program, missing all the guests in whom he's never interested anyway, since what he really watches the program for is Jon Stewart's monologue, and the other regulars, just so he can repeat the best jokes to his younger colleagues in the morning. It is, he claims, his contribution to educating the proletariat. She wonders where *The Man Show* fits in that syllabus.

"No thanks. I'm beat. Got an early call."

He raises the beer can and tips it in salutation. "G'night."

She lies in bed, unable to sleep, and finds herself wishing her husband would say stupid, David-like things, the way he used to, when he grabbed her breasts from behind and whispered, *Don't let the bedbugs bite*, the precursor to his roving fingers gently pinching her in all those places where it never hurt, not in the least.

In the living room, Jon Stewart pays homage to Madeline Albright while Frank snores. His unfinished beer sits on the coffee table, going flat.

Over the next week, Jane does not visit any of her favorite clothing haunts and blows twice her annual clothing budget on fashion at a new store. *Everything is fashion now*, she thinks as she fingers blouses that would be bodices in another century.

On Friday morning she appears at Frank's latest job, wearing a tight pair of low-slung pants that exposes her navel and a shapely lace-up blouse with just enough cleavage bared.

The site is in the thirties, a few blocks north of the Flatiron, on Twentieth, the top floor. Frank is at the northeast corner with his back to the entrance, talking on his cell. She stalks past sheet rock, metal beams, the lust of the proletariat, and grabs his butt.

Startled, he turns.

"Hey," she says.

"What are you doing here?" He speaks to the phone, "The wife just walked in, I'll call you later."

"Who were you talking to?"

"No one." The inquiry hangs and he adds, "About paint, okay?"

She backs off, defensive. "You didn't have to hang up."

"So how come you're not at work?"

"Just passing through, on my way to a meeting," she lies. "Thought maybe you'd like a break?"

He looks at her properly now and then glances up at the crew. The foreman is staring; he looks away as Frank catches his eye. "Sorry, can't. Things are kinda tense at the moment. C'mon," he says. "I'll walk you out." He shepherds her back to the elevator, clutching her arm all the way.

Like a perp walk, Jane thinks.

Her husband props open the elevator door and pecks her cheek. "Hey, don't be mad. It's just that this client's a prick. See you tonight." As the doors close he says. "By the way, isn't that outfit too young?"

Back on the streets—surely he doesn't believe she goes to *work* dressed like this?—the stares and more than a few whistles do not make her feel as naked as she felt on the way to the site. Jane wonders at the difference. In which direction is she tingling, and more to the point, does she know why?

Later, at home, Jane showers for the second time that day and braces herself against the wall as she climaxes. Everything they say about menopause is true. Lust, freed of tampons and birth control, scrambles her system like a virus, insatiable.

Hair damp, cooled now despite the heat, she calls Lily.

Jane says, "So I bounced in his face and he noticed, but all the wrong things."

Lily responds, "And you're sure he's not having an affair?"

"I don't think so. I mean, we still have sex. He comes home."

"I repeat, you're sure he's not having an affair?"

Afterwards, she wonders why she chose to call Lily, whose obsession these days is the villanelle, not men, since poetry and David are all she needs. She should have called Anna, the dancer-accountant who struts her beauty-queen stuff at male strip clubs, escorted by studs half her age, with money to burn, thus satisfying both visual and corporal needs. Of course Anna still looks if not half her age, then at least ten to twelve years younger. Accounting, Anna says, is the best head for an incorrigible playgirl like herself because it's predictable and low-stress, and balancing books *is* what life is all about. *Pretty nifty, huh?* she can hear Anna say.

Jane doesn't call Anna because she doesn't want to be regaled with tales of yet another steamy encounter with the latest stud, or to be told, again, that male flesh is willing only till age thirty-five, or at the outside, forty. *There is Viagra now,* Jane had protested the last time Anna quipped that, to which her friend replied, *I'd rather have the real thing, thank you very much.* But doesn't she also, on some deeply (or perhaps not so deeply) repressed level, wonder if it isn't *Anna* that Frank might be fucking?

Squelch that . . . this is hysteria, Jane tells herself. Anna has proven a loyal friend over the years, even more so than Lily. She wouldn't trade friendship with Anna, or Lily, for anything, and certainly not over some injustice concocted out of this onslaught of trashy desires. At least she doesn't think she would.

And suddenly Jane begins to laugh. She tries to stop but can't. What is this swell of feeling—the years of friendship, perhaps, over-taking the horizon of age—that ravages her funny bone? Nothing changes. Anna will never stop with her wacky ways and dated expressions, just as Lily will be the dreamer, a queen as she ages sweetly, trusting in poetry till the end.

That evening, Jane relegates her "too-young" clothes to the back of her closet. That night, her husband is especially amorous.

At breakfast the next morning, Frank says, "I'll be late tonight."

Jane looks up from the pile of yesterday's mail in surprise. "On a *Saturday?*" Because he won't respond, she says, "How late?"

"Don't wait up."

She has missed his return twice in less than two weeks, which hasn't escaped her notice. "What's going on?"

"Nothing. The usual. Deadlines, pain-in-the-neck client. You know."

"So you have to have dinner with the pains-in-the-neck?"

Now, he looks surprised. "What's going on with you?"

"What do you mean?"

Their eyes lock, slacken, and then, Frank softens his gaze and shrugs. "It's just that, well, you fall asleep so early now." He rises, kisses her lips in their ritual morning farewell. "But thanks anyway for last night," he says.

He doesn't even really need to know why she wasn't at work yesterday and Jane thinks, *This is it, transference,* her own adulterous longings grafted onto him. She waits impatiently for the morning to be late enough to call, and finally, unable to contain herself any longer, she calls Anna at ten thirty.

"Listen," she says to the half-awake response. "There's this guy."

Anna perks up. "*What* did you say?"

"He says I have the energy of a thirty-year-old. That's how old he is, more or less."

"How did you meet?" The voice is cautious, reserved, a far cry from the person Jane has learned to expect and accept, Anna being Lily's friend originally.

"Buying too-young clothes. He's a fashion consultant."

"Sounds gay."

"David isn't."

The line goes silent. Finally, Jane says, "I wouldn't have thought *you'd* have a problem with this."

"Hey Cucumber Gal, relax. This is Anna Banana, remember?"

"Yeah."

"So, have you, you know?"

"You mean, fuck? No." Jane pauses, then says. "Who am I kidding, he's probably gay," and then all the cool explodes and she is crying uncontrollably. Heat flashes through her, hormones scramble, and Anna says, *Hush, Jane, hush. It's okay, honey bun, it's okay, take a deep breath.*

Jane obeys her friend's command and her breathing slows as she calms. "I'm sorry, I don't know *what's* wrong," but Anna simply shushes her some more, repeating, *It's okay, you don't have to tell.*

The first time had seemed so casual, innocent, the way he gave her his card, having first impressed his hands *here, and here, and here,* his fingers straying too close to a nipple or a pubic edge, all in the name of re-arranging clothes, until her insides burned. But it had been tawdry and all wrong, going to see him on Friday. He coolly led her into his office, closed the door and then said, *Now what can I do for you?* She stared at him until he blushed, and that was when she blurted out that she needed a model, she was a painter, and the more she spoke, the more it sounded like so much babble that surely even he could see right through her that when she was done, *despite the flattery that worked and his eagerness to believe,* she fled, ashamed, not because she was horny, but because she had perverted everything she once held dear.

And this is what she tells Anna who doesn't judge, doesn't dispense advice, doesn't do anything other than listen.

After the call, Jane stands under a cold shower for at least fifteen minutes, until her fingertips wrinkle.

Monday is odd. A major scandal in the insurance industry breaks, one that has all the senior management on edge, and PowerPoint marketing presentations are the last thing on anyone's minds. So Jane has plenty of time to talk when Anna calls.

"You *sure* you're okay?" Anna asks for the second time.

"I'm sure," she replies. "Welcome to menopause."

"Funny thing, that. I was going to call and say what you said on Saturday."

Jane frowns. "What do you mean?"

"There's this guy."

So life goes on, Jane thinks, and Anna is as incorrigible as ever, but this time predictability is a relief. "So how old is this one?"

"Old. Forty, maybe even plus."

"You're slipping, kiddo."

"The thing is, we haven't had sex."

"What? He's a eunuch?"

"I'm serious. We've been on three dates, and I don't mean to see my toy boys either. Real dates. All we do is talk and then neck a little. I think this might be it, or at least, the potential of it."

For once, Jane doesn't ask for the gory—height, bodily parts, liquid assets—because she detects a strangely confessional note in her friend's voice. "Careful, you're starting to sound like Lily."

There's a pause. Then, "I thought it was you I sounded like."

"Me?"

"You're still the cat's pajamas."

Anna continues talking about this candidate for love, because it is love she means, Jane knows, it is love that she and the girls talk about even when their language is perverted by snide humor and the pose of intellect, when men are reduced to penises and abs, butts and fingers. In the end, it is always about the possibility of longevity in relating to the other, whatever form that other may take.

And before Jane knows it, it's time for her birthday.

A week before the day, Frank says at breakfast, "So which restaurant do you want to go to this year?"

"Maybe I don't want a restaurant this year."

"Flowers? Candy? What?"

She smiles. Frank has never been classically romantic, something that appealed to her from the first. "Lingerie?"

"I like you better without," he says. When she grimaces, he adds, "That's your pop's line, y'know."

"Who told you that?"

"Your mom." He rises, kisses her lips in their ritual morning farewell. "Bet you wouldn't have guessed that in a million years, huh?"

All day long, Jane hears her mother's giggled whisper to her husband. She contemplates this revisionist image of her folks and the lingering image is brighter, less painful. Perhaps, Jane thinks, it *is* time to let them go.

Shortly before eleven that night, Frank opens the fridge for a second beer, and then, to Jane's surprise, stops. He pats his stomach. "I'm putting it on, aren't I?"

"A little bit," she fibs.

"That's it," he declares. "When you start to sound like your father, I need to diet." He places an arm around her shoulders. "C'mon. It's almost time for *The Daily Show*."

They sit together on the couch. He hunts around for the remote. She holds it up, sticks it behind her back and kisses him.

He smiles. "What's that for?"

"Nothing. Just because."

Frank stares at her. "You sure you're okay?" Then, noticing, says, "How come you're in a towel? You take a shower or something?"

"It was hot."

Her husband glances at the mercury. "Seventy-two's not so hot."

He looks at her quizzically and then his expression slowly morphs into the beginnings of desire. She slides the remote between her breasts, and the towel falls away. "You like me without," she says, as she leans towards him.

AVAILABLE

"**I** mate." Jeena, slightly tipsy, glanced across the coffee table at Dennis Lam. *Dr.* Dennis Lam, visiting professor of anthropology, recently relocated from L.A.

Dennis placed his cup and saucer down on the glass surface, too rapidly, he realized too late. Porcelain clattered. "Sorry about that."

"Why should you be? It's my problem."

"I meant about the noise."

Jeena tugged at the waist of her sarong. She had tied it too tightly and perspiration welded her thighs together. It was hot for tea but it was what he wanted, saying he didn't drink much. Twenty years ago— less—she would have been suspicious of a man who wouldn't imbibe. At fifty, however, standards were history.

Dennis was speaking. "So you were saying Jeena's not really your name." He found her compelling but not attractive, and was uncertain why he'd accepted her drinks invitation. *You ought to date,* his ex-wife in California told him in May, just before he left for this year-long post in Singapore. And what *would* Dr. Katrina Bishop-Lam, chair of Women's Studies, think of Miss Jeena Mok, this hawker of real estate, who hid age spots with makeup?

"Well it is my name in Hokkien, but not spelled like that."

"You're Hokkien?"

"No, Cantonese, but there're not as many of us here."

He tried another tack. Patience was a habit he hadn't outgrown. "Why do you mate?"

"For a *vie en rose, n'est-ce pas?*" Her school French was returning with a vengeance. Academics and intellectuals stymied her; they all knew too much. Dennis was worth the effort, though, despite his five languages. *He* was available.

"Sounds like a death wish." He felt his lower lip twitch. It activated when he was nervous.

"You're being morbid. More tea?"

As she leaned forward to pour, he understood his nervousness. Jeena had dressed for cleavage—albeit underwired and assisted—and was obviously bent on seduction. He coughed. "No thanks. I must be going."

"It's not even seven thirty. Wouldn't you like some dinner?"

"Perhaps another evening. I still have a lecture to prepare tonight."

"Very well." Disappointed, Jeena saw him out. Fate had dealt her another vibrator night. With luck, the batteries wouldn't be drained.

Afterwards, undressing, she saw how the sarong creased her belly. Her undeniably softening belly. Stupid, wearing one, pretending to be some kind of "Singapore Girl," as if airline advertising should define her femininity. The dark blues and greens were a lousy contrast against her skin, making her look paler than necessary. *An anthropologist,* Diane had whispered just before introducing them, and when Jeena frowned, not entirely sure, her friend added, *You know, social culture freak.*

Yet this evening, he hadn't been at all interested in the local art and books she had rearranged for display around her flat, and asked questions instead about growing up here. He was especially curious about her *kampong.* Gone, she told him, like all the old villages, hoping he'd move on, but then he went on about what Singapore must have been like when she was a child.

"So how?" Diane asked when she rang the next day from work. She was the secretary in the business school at the university.

Jeena flipped through the new listings absently. "No use. Carcass."

"What, carcass?"

"All flesh, no blood."

"You'll see him again, yes?"

"No point."

"You know your problem? You're too impatient. Eh, boss calling, must go."

Easy for her friend to say. Diane's children were grown and her husband, who owned a travel agency, took them away on romantic weekends. Patience was fine if you were hooked. Either that or young enough not to care.

Jeena wondered why she still bothered. Other men, especially the new breed under forty, were less trouble, available for sex as they were, liking, even delighting in her unfettered lifestyle. The last mate, a Malaysian, had four years earlier forsaken her *and* his ex-family for a prolonged pilgrimage to Mecca, which should have been sufficient for any woman to be done with men. But as her now deceased father used to say, each time he beat her at chess Chinese style, Jeena was too stubborn to ever cry uncle.

Feeling guilty, Dennis invited her out to dinner the next weekend. She went because it was better than sitting home depressed. They fooled around a bit at her place afterwards, but she stopped things, saying they were both too old *not* to know each other better before giving in. The truth was, she'd been constipated for two days. He told her he agreed, and tried to sound disappointed, but truthfully, was merely relieved.

Another week passed. The Fourth of July neared.

Over the phone, Cathy Lambert said, "A barbecue, of course. Bring a date if you like, or don't. There're always plenty of spare women here, as you'll find out soon enough. It'll be quite informal."

"I'll try to make it," Dennis replied. Cathy was a pre-marital ex-flame. The Lamberts were old friends of theirs, his and Katrina's.

"Don't try, Dennis. Make it. I promised Katrina we'd look after you."

"I'll try."

He supposed he ought to be grateful that of all the consular postings in the world, Jim Lambert had managed to land Singapore just at this moment. The Lamberts stuck, the way Katrina did. There was their daughter, of course, but his ex-wife offered an amiable link even after her re-marriage to Walt. Mating and re-mating. Incestuous ritual.

I mate.

Jeena's defiant attitude posited an availability, albeit a potentially difficult one. She didn't look fifty, could pass for her late thirties, but wasn't that just the way it was with all Asians? Katrina wouldn't agree. She said Dennis looked much older than his forty-seven years, a result, she insisted, of diet. Katrina was *Fit for Life*, her bible for the trek towards old age.

The problem was—the problem always was—Jeena wasn't his type.

What do you want, Dennis? You've got to learn to be honest with yourself. Five years later, still hearing Katrina as she left him.

Okay, so Katrina was brunette and studious, but sexy, while Cathy was a vivacious blonde and perky, but certainly not studious. Two completely different bodies, voices, ways of being loved. Each had been his type once, as had others since. But that was before he subsumed desire to its present simmer.

Bring Jeena, he decided. It would be easier than fielding the spares. Besides, Jim would like her. At their age, small consolations were hard to come by.

Diane combed through her split ends, cradling the handset in the crook of her arm. "So if carcass why go?"

Jeena peered at a fax, trying to make out the phone number. Were her eyes also headed towards a similar descent as her breasts? Her nail scratched a crimson streak across the paper. "Business contacts. Might also meet someone else."

"Since when male extras?"

"Never know."

"Admit it. You like him. Good on the horizontal, huh?"

"No idea."

"You? *He*llo, Mrs. Robinson-Mok. Can*not* believe."

Jeena winced. The problem with long friendships, from kindergarten no less, was that nothing remained sacred. Also, in Diane's lurid imagination, one minor moment of madness—ancient history already even before the last mate—had exploded exponentially into an ongoing trend. She said. "Appointment. Late."

Her friend refused to relent. "So how?"

"*Ai-yor,* he *is* Cantonese. *Simahn* as well." There, that would satisfy Diane, who didn't believe well-mannered Cantonese males existed, given the Hong Kong migrants peopling Singapore these days at an alarming rate. This way, she needn't tell her that this one was different, especially since she couldn't quite say why. Besides, she was fed up of explaining herself over that inexplicable subject of men.

When they arrived at the Lamberts', Jeena knew she had struck the right balance between casual and smart. Years of the party circuit taught her: Americans dressed for success, the Canadians for decency, Europeans to seduce, while Brits wore comfort as style. Asians followed the primary flow. Jeena guessed, correctly, that most of the unattached Singaporean females would be young. Had Dennis been Caucasian, she would have declined the invitation.

Of course, she observed, he might as well be, this "banana" who talked baseball and U.S. politics. He was fortunately not one of the giants, and she, stunted at four foot ten, did not feel uncomfortable beside him. Tapping her foot in time to the jazz trio hired for the occasion, she glanced around the heavily expatriate crowd. From across the pool, one local, a marginally inebriated former client, waved. His wife, who had been Jeena's college classmate, did not.

Svengali oozed past. That wasn't his name but it was what everyone called the fast-moving Sikh banker. Everyone local. His eyebrows arched towards Dennis. "So where's he putting up? With you?"

Dennis, engrossed in defending the Braves—his home team, as he later enlightened her—had not heard.

Jeena stuck out her tongue. "Don't be rude."

Svengali puckered. "Darling, I wouldn't dream. Just checking out your prospects," and he was off to harass another intimate.

She smiled in spite of him. A long time ago, they had engaged in a brief, torrid encounter, during school days, when commitment was to life, not love. It had been daring, surrendering virginity before her sixteenth year. Diane had gasped, wide-eyed, and then wanted to know every minute, every detail, right down to the brand of condom. "Like heaven," Jeena had reported. "Better than being in love."

Now, he was still fighting over custody, while she... just what was she?

A twenty-something siren appeared, champagne flute in one hand and a cigarette in the other, posing for all the world as if her body were eternal. She slinked past Dennis, who looked. Turning to Jeena, he asked, "had enough?" His plate sported a half-eaten burger.

Her own was clean. She had demolished three chicken wings, a burger, and two hot dogs, without the buns. "Is that all you're eating?"

"I'm not very hungry," he replied, untruthfully. But he was reminded of his mother, who (unlike the women who peopled his bed), focused exclusively on nourishment.

"You don't like barbecue?"

"Not really."

Perhaps soup noodles, she considered. He *was* Chinese, after all, even if formed in exile among the barbarians. Shrugging off hesitation, she offered, "Want some *tong mien?*"

"With fish balls?"

"And pig skin too if you like."

He felt slightly delirious. "Lead the way."

The open-air hawker stall, situated out towards the East Coast near Changi, was quiet during this odd hour before dusk. He ate everything she ordered, greedily, comforted by the familiar aromas and tastes of childhood. Of oily soups bubbling with offal, tripe, pig trotters, fish heads, and other indelicacies. Of deep-fried doughnut sticks to soak up rice porridge at breakfast. Of unclean woks, flavored by layers of cooking wiped into the surface, never washed. Of cockles and clams soaked in garlic and shreds of red peppers, on special occasions only in his native, landlocked Atlanta.

Katrina's cuisine—healthy vegan, steamed, with every variety of tofu—was edible but weird.

Sated, he stared out towards the water. "This was all wide open once, wasn't it?"

"Sure." She burped quietly. The *choi sum* counteracted her earlier consumption of flesh. Barbecues were fine, except for the lack of cooked, leafy greens.

He wiped his mouth with a handkerchief. "Do you like living in Singapore?"

She glimpsed the character of his surname, monogrammed at the corner of his handkerchief. Funny how Americans spent their money. "What a strange question."

"Why is it strange?"

"This is my home. Even if I lived somewhere else, I'd always come back."

His lower lip twitched. "Sorry, I was being presumptuous."

"Now, *that's* strange." He was, she knew, very American, but not offensively so. His appetite, on the other hand, made her smile.

He gestured across the highway. "Those apartment blocks. I imagine they're worth a fortune."

"Thirty-five hundred for a two-bedroom, and rising. I rented one to an American musician last week." Noting the calculation in his eyes, she added, "About twenty-three hundred U.S."

"Musicians must do all right here."

"Everyone does."

His own lease, paid for by the university, made this stint affordable. He reached for his wallet, but she waved it away.

"My treat," she said.

"I ate most of the food."

"You pay for the next one, okay? An expensive one." She laughed then stopped abruptly, thinking, wrong for him, this joke Svengali would have appreciated. She rubbed the side of her nose, a habit when nervous.

He burst out laughing. "That's a good one."

When she dropped him off at his place—he had considered, and quickly rejected a car once he fully comprehended the exorbitant cost—Dennis invited her in.

She shook her head, surprising herself. "Early call. Some other time." It wasn't strictly true, but it was close enough.

He leaned over and kissed her. Their tongues joined briefly.

Later, he could not shake her taste, even after toothpaste. Chives and pig skin lingered. The night air was cool in the wake of the rains. As his body eased into sleep, it brushed against desire, turning the simmer up to medium-high.

Within the week, he saw her again. He suggested an expensive Italian restaurant on Orchard, but she nixed that and brought him to a small, out of-the-way place where the Italian owner selected and prepared a fixed menu, including the wine, for his patrons each evening. Dennis drank the Amarone, delighting in its velvet languor, unconcerned by the tremors of intoxication.

That night, Jeena stopped at his place. She was wrapped around him on the sofa when Katrina called. An emergency. Their daughter.

She tried not to eavesdrop, and leafed through the *Straits Times*, which she'd already read that morning.

When Dennis returned, some twenty minutes later, he said. "Sorry about that."

"Is everything all right?"

"No."

She waited through his silence.

Finally, "I'm sorry, it's difficult." His voice faltered.

"Would you like me to leave?"

He stared at her, grateful for the muted curiosity. "I have to make a trip back. Alaina, our daughter, was arrested in a club raid. Ecstasy."

His lower lip was on a rampage. "She's a freshman in college," he added.

Jeena rubbed the side of her nose. Her last mate, before heading for Mecca, had bailed out an ex-wife who, allegedly, had seduced a minor, their daughter's boyfriend. After a pause, "Well, at least she won't be caned. Not over there."

"No." He smiled. Fatherhood felt distinctly lighter.

"Come," she said. "I'll take you for *siu ye.*" It was almost eleven, late enough for seconds.

Dennis breathed deep. It was good not to have to discuss this further. "When in doubt, eat?"

"Something like that."

"So *is* he available or not?"

Her friend was beginning to sound like a broken record. Jeena waved off the inevitable and replied, "Maybe. We'll see."

Diane shook her left hand vigorously. Two hues of green were drying nicely on her nails. "It's been, what, five, almost six weeks? Long-term for you."

"During which I've seen him, what, four and a half times?"

"What, half?"

"Took him to the airport. I told you."

"Oh, yeah."

"Your mind's a sieve."

"Isn't your heart? So, you done it yet?"

Jeena rolled her eyes. "Goodbye."

"Getting all coy in your old age, eh? Hey, don't forget call Simon Eng. He needs a place. Maybe girlfriend too now that his wife's thrown him out. *He* hasn't got kids."

"Goodbye!" She hung up with a loud click.

Last night, Dennis had called from L.A. Just to say hi. It had been a long time—years—since anyone had sprung for long-distance. It was obscurely pleasant, like catching whiffs of girlhood, a time before men occupied such wholly valuable mental space, rent-free.

There were things that Diane, married straight out of school, would never understand. On the subject of mating, there was a point past which there was nothing left to tell.

Amazingly quick, clearing immigration at Changi International. Dennis found his bag waiting at the carousel the minute he emerged, an unexpected welcome back.

Pale blue taxi, speeding along the East Coast. Sun and trees. Katrina frantic. Sky and sea. Alaina crying, promising *never again Daddy, I'm really sorry.* Katrina and he and Alaina. Walt, childless, standing by dumbly. *Thanks for being so available, Dennis,* the mother of his child said, when the worst was over.

Anger abated in the face of remorse, Dennis found the trip "home" less unpleasant than he had dreaded. He didn't know what possessed him to call Jeena. Perhaps the civilized discomfort of sleeping in his own guest room—Katrina had gotten the house—made him want to stake some claim. Territorial, he decided, even in temporary shelters. Humans created ritual for sanity or worse.

Back in L.A. on the way to the airport, he mentioned Jeena again to Alaina.

His daughter said, "That's such a pretty name." She kept her eyes on the road. "I'm glad there's someone for you, too."

"Well, I don't know about that yet."

"What's to know? You either like her or you don't."

They were nearing the terminal. Alaina dodged the traffic confidently. He watched her, proud.

"Well, we're here." She pecked his cheek.

"Jeena mates," he repeated.

"You keep saying that." Alaina leaned her elbow against the wheel. "To mate," she began, imitating his voice and style at a lecture, "is to equal, rival, vie, or cope with. The dictionary is your best friend in the language of uncertainty."

"Smart ass."

"I *am* your daughter. Daddy, go for the home run."

"Just like that, huh?"

"Uh huh. And maybe a little ecstasy."

"Watch it." He rubbed his chin. His lower lip was still. "You know, she's a bit like your grandma."

"Oh, really?" His daughter frowned, recalling too many gruesome meals in Atlanta that shouldn't even be fed to pigs. "Whatever. At least you'll eat."

He laughed. Summer's lease held promise. "At least."

BEASTLY TALES

CRYING WITH AUDREY HEPBURN

for WILLIAM WARREN

YEAH the ring's for real. Why would I pretend about that? So what is it you want to know, kid? That I wouldn't be "dancing" if not for Ron? That things might be different if he hadn't pulled his vanishing act? Ron never introduced me to his family. Said they didn't give two shits about him after his mom re-married, so why stay in touch? Guess I can't blame him.

Of course, I'm hardly one to talk.

Still, though. Might have been nice to have some American in-laws even if they'd never come to Manhattan.

Okay kid, write this down.

Mother cried over Audrey Hepburn movies.

"She's so elegant," she sniffed, "and helpless. No wonder men look after her."

On television, *Sabrina* was approaching its illogical conclusion. It was Saturday, February 29, 1964, the night of my father's fifty-ninth birthday. I was fourteen. *A-Ba* was at a dinner hosted by my three older brothers. We didn't go because of Audrey, but also because Mother said fifty-nine wasn't a big deal, and that my brothers and their wives were wasting time sucking up to *A-Ba*, hoping to get his money.

"I don't know what you're crying about," I said. "It's just a movie. It isn't real."

My mother dried her eyes with a silk handkerchief. "It wouldn't hurt you to soften up a bit and be a little more elegant."

Mother's Eurasian, but if you look at her face front, she passes for Chinese. Exotic perhaps, but Chinese. Her mother was an American missionary's daughter who married a wealthy Cantonese trader against her parents' wishes. My father is a Cantonese businessman who makes and sells soy sauce—Yangtze Soy—when he's not boozing. Whenever his commercial airs, the one where sauce cascades down cleavage to the opening of Grieg's piano concerto, Mother switches off the television in disgust.

"Here," she said, handing me her crochet work. "Put this away, please."

I complied and escaped to my bedroom, grateful to surface above the vale of tears.

Elegance. Facing the mirror in third position, I studied my feet. Six and a half and still growing; already, it was hard finding shoes my size. Mother would die if she knew I danced all the boys' parts. "Ballet will help you be more graceful," she insisted when she started me up nine years earlier. "It's important for young ladies to be graceful because gentlemen like that." Mother's graceful. She has jet-black hair, large eyes, high cheekbones and a figure like Audrey's. I could imagine her in Humphrey Bogart's arms, dancing to "Isn't It Romantic." Mother loves to dance, but *A-Ba* can't foxtrot to save his life.

Sabrina is such a silly story. Bogart and Holden are these unlikely brothers of a wealthy Long Island family. Audrey's the chauffeur's daughter who has a crush on Holden. She disappears off to cooking school in Paris, returns grown up and sophisticated, which is when he finally notices her. But the family doesn't want her marrying Holden, so Bogart turns on the charm, intending to pay Audrey off. Instead, he falls for her, and they end up getting married. The End.

My hair's limp, and a faded mousy brown. I have Mother's height and *A-Ba's* frazzled eyebrows, beady eyes, and ugly mouth. I look *pathetically* Eurasian. My brothers inherited the best of my parents: they pass for Chinese and all made it over five foot eight, a real asset among Hong Kong men. Leftover blood coursed through me, the accident, seventeen years after the last boy. Good thing I was a girl. That way, Mother fussed over me in her old age, and didn't even mind the way I looked.

In the living room, Bogart and Audrey were sailing off to their Parisian honeymoon in black and white. Personally, I couldn't see what she saw in him. I would have taken Holden any day, philanderer though he was. After all, there was no guarantee what Bogart would be like after Paris.

But kid, I'm getting too old for this. What? You think Ron happened yesterday? Audrey Hepburn died; that's what happened yesterday. Papers said cancer. Too bad Ron's not here. We'd have honored her passing together.

So you want to hear the rest of this story or not?

On her way home from lunch with friends the next afternoon, my mother was killed by a hit-and-run driver.

"She was running across the street again," my father shouted. "Always running!"

He had seldom been as angry. *A-Ba's* an ugly man who was once better looking. Smashed his face against a cracked toilet bowl when he was drunk one night, and emergency did a lousy job on his jowl. In his fury, his gnarled, contorted face resembled a lion's head in the dance—a shiny red-and-gold mask with fierce eyes.

"It was an accident," I said. "The police said so. Besides, the driver should have stopped."

"Always running," he muttered.

Can't recall much about the funeral. My three brothers did the adult things and said very little to me. We're virtually strangers, since they were gone by the time I was born. I wanted to scream at everyone to shut up and stop crying. I didn't cry. My thoughts zigzagged from the driver who left my mother on the road to die; to my father, who never spent time with her; to Audrey, dancing in the moonlight in the arms of Bogart, the ugly industrialist, the man who would look after her for the rest of her life as Sabrina. Only in celluloid, not in Hong Kong.

Hey kid, I'm on. We do five shows Friday night. You're going to wait? Suit yourself. Back in fifteen, max.

How did he get me started? Asked about the ring, that's how. This one's different. Got a little class. Been in a few times, always buys me a drink. Looks at me when he speaks. Most guys can't. All they see is... well, you know.

Ron couldn't even watch me dance, never mind this act. But if it weren't for my little specialty, I couldn't keep this job, not now. Occasionally, he'd wait outside, even in the snow, before things got bad. "Time Square's no place for a girl after dark," he'd say, whenever he walked me home. Afterwards, we'd watch movies together till sunrise.

I miss that.

Vegetables? Funny? I suppose they are. There was the cigar, until some joker lit it. Scorched thighs hurt. Like the boss says, every act needs to change. Cucumbers taste better anyway.

Oh so now you want to know what happened next? You're the funny one, kid.

Six months later, A-Ba sent me away to an all-girl boarding school in Connecticut.

"You've been begging to go to the States," he said over my protests. "I've made all the arrangements. Besides, I can't look after you."

He hadn't touched any of Mother's stuff since the funeral. I wanted to find a keepsake among her silks and jewelry, but didn't dare without his permission. Being the only girl, it was my right to have the first go. Once I was gone, my sisters-in-law would ransack all her beautiful things, and there'd be nothing left for me.

I sulked my way to Connecticut.

Didn't like the school. We weren't allowed late-night TV. Despite the rules, we sneaked out after dark to meet boys. My classmates were in competition to lose their virginity. I won on my sixteenth birthday, easy. You don't have to be either graceful or beautiful in the back seat of a car. Being the only foreigner added to the freak factor. Anyway, it's not like those boys would bring me home.

I wrote home, dutifully, once a month. My brothers I never heard from. *A-Ba* only wrote brief notes with money, once each semester.

Mother would have written me long, gossipy letters, full of movies and news of society friends. If she'd seen an Audrey, her words might have flown. Mother survived on sentiment. She used to say, "One day, I'm taking you to New York where we'll do breakfast at Tiffany's. We'll buy the diamonds for your wedding there." When it all got too much, I'd shout, "Mother, don't be silly! Who'd marry *me*?" And she would hold me tight, tears rolling down her cheeks, promising, "Trust me, my darling, someone will. Someone will."

I never wasted time crying.

Fantasy home. That's what this club is. Guys come in for escape or relief because they can't make it. *A-Ba* wasn't like them. He had Mother because he was successful. Problem was, she needed someone classier. Wasn't his fault. Other than his temper, he wasn't all bad. It's just that you can't manufacture class the way you can soy sauce.

Maybe I came along too late and caught a dismal closing act. They must have had a better life once.

I didn't talk about family to anyone.

Summer after graduation, I finally was allowed home. In Connecticut, it was possible not to think about her or her miserable life with A-Ba. But home, without Mother, was worse than being kept away at school.

In late August, Wait Until Dark made it to Hong Kong's cinemas. It was petrifying, watching a blind Audrey stumble around, stalked and terrorized like prey. I'm glad Mother didn't have to watch. Fear isn't romantic.

Listen kid, you want to tell this story? I'm getting to the Ron part. Didn't you learn in your writing school that stories need history, plot, suspense? Character flaws? Otherwise the beginning muddles to the middle and you thank god it's The End.

Southern Connecticut State was a bore, but it was better than high school.

The boys were less frantic. I majored in something. All I cared about was dance. My feet though! They felt way too big, having ballooned to a seven and a half.

Fall of sophomore year, Ron Andrews danced into my life.

His troupe was performing "Dance Nostalgia." Astaire routines. Porter, Kern, Gershwin. Ron did this solo soft shoe number. The grand finale was him leaping onto a straight-back chair, tipping it over, and sliding towards the apron's edge on his knees. I jumped up, shouted "bravo," not caring what anyone thought. Maybe I started something, or maybe he was just that good, because the whole audience rose in a swell, cheering.

Later, backstage, Ron stood there, a towel round his neck. In his T-shirt and tights, one leg cocked on a stool, he looked like a blond William Holden. People congratulated; voices rose in a frenzy. He wasn't very tall, but there in the center of all that adulation, he was a giant.

When we were introduced, I couldn't help gushing. "You were incredible. Absolutely, amazingly marvelous!" He smiled, nodded in acknowledgement, and that was that.

Back at the dorm that night, I cried myself silly. It was such a weird sensation. I mean, I didn't know the guy to save my life, and crying wasn't my thing.

The next day, I went along to audition for their troupe's summer stock.

I was a good, but not brilliant, dancer. The point was, it didn't matter a whole lot whether or not I performed. Other students had rehearsed for weeks, desperate to make the cut. My friend Sara co-opted me as her "male" partner. I'd agreed, but that was before Ron. Of course, I couldn't very well back out now, not when the show had to go on.

"Smile, will you?" Sara hissed, just before we made our entrance. "Don't be such a dog face. Think Astaire."

We did "Dancing in the Dark." Sara's this tiny brunette, graceful as sin. In her white ball gown, fitted to her gorgeous figure, she was stunning. I was in tux tails, my hair pinned tightly in a net, a moustache pasted on for effect, feeling absurd. Sara's a strong dancer, but she hams things up too much. Every dip swooped a bit too low; every turn was overdone. Friends applauded, but I knew we weren't much above passable.

Later, while removing makeup, I looked up in the mirror and saw him. He wasn't as young as he appeared on stage. He pressed both hands down on my shoulders and studied my face. "Do you ever dance the lady's part?" His voice resonated. Baritone.

Nodding and shaking my head simultaneously, I stammered, "Sometimes."

"Come on then." Taking my hand, he led me on stage. In my tux shirt and tights, I looked ridiculous, but Ron didn't seem to care as we stood side by side, arms outstretched, my hand in his. I was the taller, and nervous.

"Dancing in the Dark" came on.

"Follow me," he commanded.

My feet flowed. It was better than magic, because all of me danced, guided by heaven and his lead. When the music faded, it segued to "In the Mood." His hands gripped my waist and he swung me in the air. A perfect partner, confident without being bossy, leading without stifling my movements. When we finished, the applause went on for a long, long time.

On stage, I smiled at him, exhilarated, my heart pounding from exhaustion. Ron had barely broken a sweat. He pulled me towards him in a final twirl. "What's your name?" he asked. His eyes were a deep blue-green, as deep as the ocean, only deeper.

I quit school and followed him to New York. He was thirty, the senior member in the troupe.

"A dancer?!" My father screamed over intercontinental telephone wires. "You're living with a *baak gwai* dancer? What are you, crazy?"

"But you married one. Or at least, a half *baak gwai*. I just wanted you to know."

"You'll get no more money from me."

"I don't need your money. I can work."

"Doing what? Shining his shoes? What do you expect to make without a college degree?"

I hung up. Ron never got to speak to him.

That was the last time I communicated with my family. What do you suppose Mother would have said?

I remind you of your sister? Another funny face, huh? Everything comes back to family, kid. We all start there, even if we end up someplace remote. Like Ron. Despite his stepdad, who beat him up and hadn't a clue, calling him a fag and all, he still thought about his mom. Oh, he'd never admit it, but I knew. Every Mother's Day, he used to cry in his sleep, like clockwork.

Ron and I got married six months later.

Life was great. He scored tickets to Broadway shows because he knew people in the business. Ron had tons of friends. He was like the sun in this solar system, burning bright, in whose orbit everyone sparkled and spun. He found places to perform, way off Broadway, all across the country, even in Alaska, while other dancers waited tables or collected welfare. "I've got to dance," he said. "Doesn't matter how or where."

We did dance contests and exhibitions for money whenever he was in between real gigs. Other than that, we didn't work together much. His act, the dance of his heart, was solo. Money was tight, but that never mattered because I loved him and we were rent controlled. He used to work a lot then, going to every audition, trying for the big break. Such energy! "Disco won't last," he predicted. "It'll bore itself to death. You wait and see."

We talked. I told him all about my mother, about my Tiffany's "wedding," about her crying with Audrey Hepburn. Sometimes, talking made me weepy. He'd hold me until I calmed. Blood talk, he called it. Healing that scabs the pain.

After two years in New York, I took a job as a typist and filing clerk. It was way more lucrative than dancing and had health insurance. Ron didn't want me to do it. "What about your career? You're a good dancer when you try."

"You dance," I replied. "I'll feed us. Anyway, we'll still do the contests."

He picked me up, effortlessly. "Lazybones. Always wanting the easy way."

Up in the air, I laughed. "Life doesn't have to be tough all the time."

"Then, what would you say if I tossed you out the window?" He swung me horizontal and held me there.

"Don't you dare."

He gave up when he saw I wouldn't budge. That was Ron: never made me do anything against my will. As long as he was our star, I was happy.

Besides, I liked shining his tap shoes. His feet were small and elegant, as if they'd been bound and sculpted to dance from the womb.

This rock? It's fake. You think I'd be dancing if it wasn't?

After I heard about Audrey yesterday, I hauled myself up to Tiffany's. Some things you just do. Colorless things, diamonds. Don't know what Mother saw in them. At least she loved me in her own silly way. Ron was right about that. He was right about a lot, especially love. He said deep down, my father loved me because I was his flesh and blood. His own father had been a dancer, but died when Ron was eight. So he knew all about what he called the "empty spaces of the heart."

But Ron was wrong about A-Ba. All these years and he's never once tried to find me, I don't think.

When Audrey Hepburn made her comeback in '76, it was all Ron and I talked about.

We'd missed her. I'd seen every one of her movies, in memory of Mother, but Ron liked her too. She looked pretty good for her age. You know, if you look at her face front, she could almost pass for Eurasian.

That year, I dyed my hair and eyebrows coal black, and cut a young-Audrey bob. Ron said it made me look exotic. All the guys at work noticed. That was also when I started wearing makeup every day.

Funny stuff, makeup. One reason I never took performing too seriously was because I didn't like all that stage goo. Ron was tireless and careful about his; he needed to hide the lines. Mother wore makeup like it wasn't there, long before the natural look. Her foundation and powder blended into the skin tones of her neck, unlike women who didn't match their complexion properly, and looked as if they'd severed and re-attached their heads. She painted on eyeliner with a brush, rapidly, expertly, like an artist, but never used eye shadow. "Women with blue lids," she declared disdainfully, "look frostbitten."

Letting Ron pluck my eyebrows was a revelation. "You see, you do have eyes," he said. "They were hidden by all that bushy fuzz." With a little eyeliner, my eyes became wider, brighter, more open.

I smiled at people now, instead of looking down all the time. I even admitted my feet were *not* too big. As Ron said, seven and a half is an average size in America. I began wearing stylishly nostalgic dresses from secondhand stores. Ron loved my quirky new look. "Lady fair," he declaimed, "you put the stars and models to shame!"

That was the happiest time of my entire life. I felt elegant, even graceful.

Trust me, I don't talk to just anyone. It's not like I tell *every* writer who asks. What, you didn't think you were the first, did you?

I started dancing here because welfare ran out. After getting laid off, it was great not working for awhile. Like vacation. I loved playing housewife and not having to answer to anyone. Ron said not to worry about getting another job, something would turn up. He even suggested auditioning. But at twenty-eight, I felt silly competing with the kids. Wouldn't say that to him though. Why hurt his feelings?

In the beginning, I just used to dance. I tried a strip tease, but it wasn't a success. As the boss says, you have to have tits for that, and I wasn't about to go silicon. So I stuck to the cage, or pole, because gams I've got. I'd come up with costumes for variety, like a see-through cheongsam with the waist-high slit, the Suzie Wong look? Oh, well, I guess you are too young. Anyway, that was a big favorite. The act didn't come about till much later.

I don't remember exactly when Ron and I stopped dancing together.

What is it you want to know, kid?

Shortly after Audrey's comeback, things started going badly for Ron.

He didn't let on at first, laughing off problems and carrying on as if he were eternally on stage. First year, his agent was slow about returning calls. He talked about getting another. Then, even friends in the business stopped returning calls, and his agent only had truly awful gigs, like the commercial where he had to wear a cow costume and tap dance around these giant milk bottles. I told him it was just the times, that the economy sucked and things were bound to get better. There were still occasional road shows in Alabama or some-place. We'd saved a little money, which was enough to live on because I was a careful housekeeper, although Ron teased, calling me stingy.

Then I lost my job, it was tough finding another, and yadda yadda, you know the rest. But back then on 42nd Street, they always needed fresh girls.

By daylight, Times Square was seedy, but not awful. Reminded me of Wanchai back home. When I was thirteen, I used to hang around Lockhart Road after school. The *mama-sans* would stand around posing, fat old broads with painted masks and too-tight cheongsams. They'd cat call passing American sailors, pointing at the curtained doorways. It was like watching a show, somewhere very far off Broadway, right at the edge of the grid. I gawked and giggled with my friends until they shooed us away.

Don't know where I found the guts to walk into the biggest joint that day. Looking good helped, and I could still dance. They hired me right off. I was nervous the first night. It was a Tuesday. Place was dead except for a bunch of geezers in the corner. "Pretend you're in a movie," one of the girls told me. "That way, you're not flesh."

Ron was mad, but kept quiet because we needed the cash. After the first three months or so, he relaxed when he saw I always came straight home. "Just a job, I guess," he'd say. I never expected him to dance, never breathed even the slightest hint though he would have been terrific. He was way too fine for all this.

If only he'd kept going.

The kid. He looks a little like Ron.

You're leaving town tomorrow? Getting married?

Ron went away, oh, ages ago. Before he left home that winter afternoon, he claimed he was tired of the whole damned thing, said I would have been better off with Bogart. I didn't get what he meant because I was running, late for work.

In the morning, they found his tap shoes on the Brooklyn Bridge, his wallet and wedding band inside them. All I remember is, it was the day before he turned forty.

See you, kid. Good luck with the writing and all. Hey, what's your name? I'll look for your book some day.

So that's the end. No one listens after the story's over.

I cried myself to sleep for months afterwards. Ron kept me going, gave me hope, made me feel I was as good as any star despite my life. "Audrey Hepburn doesn't hold a candle to you," he'd say. He filled up my heart with so much love I thought it would burst. What more could a girl want?

Crying over Ron made me remember Mother. They would have adored each other. There were days I thought about going to join them both. Every night, I'd get up on stage and dance to whistles and catcalls, or the dead space of labored breathing, and I'd be okay. But away from here, alone in daylight, the space in my heart became immensely empty and bare. Tears cascaded from some mysterious source, against my will, until the day ended and night returned again.

And then one day, I'm not sure when or why, I just stopped crying.

Dancing's been a kind of life. You get used to it. It's better than hammering away at a noisy electric, mucking with carbons, hoping the cartridge won't run out halfway. Plus no office politics. Girls who dance, they'll be friends or leave you alone, whatever you want. Independent types. I like that.

The boss was good about things. Kept me on after Ron died, mostly because he felt bad for me. But business is business, and let's face it, I was over thirty and this place *is* about fresh girls. So I came up with the cigar. He was skeptical, but gave it a whirl. I was a big draw. After the lighting incident, we moved on to vegetables. These were fine except for daikons because those taste bad raw. But the boss was right. Variety *is* spice, so out I strutted on spikes, hiked up the skirt, sucked in, spat out, and caught each tubular from between the legs, shoved each one between the lips, and crunched, hard, the pale, peeled daikon being the finale. Like juggling, with dance.

When I turned forty a few years back, the boss and girls gave me this big party. I look pretty good for my age. You can't see the lines unless you look close. Makeup works. The girls come and go while I hang on. You have to keep going.

The act keeps me going. These days, we need to be careful. There's less you can get away with. Mood of the times; a conservative feel's in the air. That'll blow over, like disco. Besides, it's time to think about retiring. Economy's improving. Ballroom's hot again and there are gigs at shopping malls or the Y. I could do those. You don't need to be either young or brilliant to fox trot or jitterbug. All you need is a partner.

It was a silly way for Ron to exit. I would have supported us forever. He was all the home I wanted, even on those days when he couldn't get out of bed. If only he hadn't given up. He would always have been my star.

Show time. Feet hurt.

Funny Face is on later. That's *my* favorite. Yes it *is* just an earlier *Fair Lady*, except she does the actual singing. Astaire's supposed to be this famous fashion photographer who turns plain-Jane book-worm Audrey into a top model. Naturally, they fall in love, and their wedding day is the grand finale.

Astaire dances delightfully, and Audrey wears the most delicious dresses. Story's hilarious. I love it where she's all in black, among the Parisian pseudo-intellectuals, dancing past their stony faces. And the corny ending makes me laugh. Fred's way too old for her, of course, and the plot's quite impossible. But in the movies, none of this matters, because it's always a perfect match, made only the way those can be, in heaven, and never on earth.

LADY DAY

I**T'S** the stiff collar—tightly buttoned, covering the entire neck—that draws the eye to the lips. Makeup, high heels, and the walk are second nature; thighs—firm, barely, silkily there—flash through the fitting cheongsam's side slits. Their glances, discreet or longing, slide up the leg, over the hip, away from the front and round back to where my black hair falls, like some endangered feline's tail, long enough to sit on. I pass as easily here in Amsterdam as in New York, with less complications.

Medical complications are something else. Outwardly, nothing's changed, not yet. But inwardly, I feel different, and know that the onset about which I've been warned has probably begun. There are things inside you can't deny, and the best physicians and all the money in the world won't yield the desired return.

Right now, though, I'll live these nights, playacting a little longer. Tonight's the "dynamic duo." Double jeopardy, double the return. It's their third transaction this week, the last night of their little "business trip" to the continent. They're having the time of their life. Those boys obviously like my wares.

What I miss, what I'll never get back, is the rush of control, *the game of being her*. Running the whole show on my terms. Many returned. Repeat business; Bernard taught me well.

Waan yuen, as Daddy might have said. Party's over. No one to blame, not even Hewitt.

But most of all, I've missed daylight.

The day Hewitt called, however, I was getting a little tired of the day job, imagining perhaps things could still change if I had just that much more money to retire completely from the life, which is how all this started.

It was early on an April morning, two years prior, how quickly life moves on. Hewitt Chan. That's how he introduced himself. He sounded young.

He gave three references: Bernard, the East Coast ivy league business professor; Kevin, the CEO of a Texas oil and gas concern; and Mahmoud, the Saudi prince.

"How do you know Kevin?" I asked. Kevin pays me in stock of relatively unknown companies and always says when to sell. The gains usually amount to ten times or more the purchase price. Years ago, he taught me to trade commodities. Kevin's the reason I have this sizeable retirement portfolio and money for private doctors. Him I actually liked and in some ways regret losing the most.

Hewitt replied. "I interviewed him."

"You're an, ah... journalist?"

"Do you want this contract or not?"

"I placed this call?"

I almost said no, and sometimes still wished I had, but business had been slow, so I told him I'd check, and called Kevin, who was in transit and unavailable. Because it was the hour Riyadh, and Mahmoud, rested, I tried Bernard next. He was in class.

Hewitt called less than ten minutes later. "So did I check out?"

"Tight schedule?"

"Lady, are you selling or not?"

I remained polite. "Mr. Chan, you're welcome to take your business elsewhere."

"Money's no object," he said quickly.

"This is not just about money."

"It *always* is."

"We'll call you," I replied, and hung up.

This was annoying me *way* more than it should. *Control.* I inhaled, finished my coffee and signed on the net.

Hewitt Chan turned out to be a writer for magazines like *Forbes* and *Fortune.* I skimmed his interviews of Kevin Leighton and Carter

Mahmoud. The stories were profiles of them and their companies. Maybe I was just having a bad day.

At around ten, Bernard called to vouch for him. "Go easy. This one doesn't play hardball." He laughed.

"Was he one of your students?"

"Sweetheart, how would I remember?"

I wanted to ask then why was he acting as a reference, but he had to run.

Although Bernard Jantzen's a long-standing client, I don't much care for him. He wants the kind of rough stuff I don't normally handle, and his Cubans stink up my office. But he taught me most of what I know about running a business profitably, which gave me my independence for a long while. So him I indulged.

I called Hewitt Chan back. "Okay, no problem. See you at two." I gave the address of the temporary executive suite where I've had an arrangement for years. They think I'm an international financial consultant because I say I am, dress like one, and never discuss my clients.

"Not that one," he said. "Your private office."

"What's this? Exclusive?"

"A big one."

Exclusives run up to three hours and include entry. These take place at my office with the choice of a conference table, an office desk, and the reception sofa.

Oh, I forgot to say I used to only work day johns, at the office; by then, they always came to me, and not the other way around. Carter nicknamed me "Lady Day" years ago because he adores Billie Holiday, and it was a handle that stuck. Being a morning person, this matches my disposition, and an office is low overhead. No beds to make or sheets to wash; office furniture wipes clean. Plus I can get back to trading. On the date I claimed as my thirtieth birthday, Carter Mahmoud *gave* me use of a downtown space in a renovated building near Wall Street, for which I only paid running costs. *My* "private office," in exchange for priority services. Having few inhibitions,

Carter fully delighted in "strange fruit" as he sometimes named me. It was the *nicest* gift. I hated giving that up.

But I digress.

The man who met me that afternoon was as young as his voice—twenty-six or seven I'd guess—and Chinese of the domestic variety, probably Cantonese. He was built like a runner or cyclist, lean and long. Sweet face, nice smile, but his chin was rather too round for his face and had his ears been a tad longer, he'd be Spock. He was nervous, which I hadn't expected.

"Welcome," I said.

His eyes skittered around the office. "So," he said, trying to look cool. "Where do we start?"

"Your call, darling."

At five that afternoon—I don't do overtime—he stood naked by the conference table and cleared his throat. "I'm a little short," he said, showing me his wallet.

Stiff me, would he? Time to stop being polite. "Cut the crap."

He smirked. "Call the police."

"Brat."

"What're you going to do? Spank me?"

I did. Despite my small frame, I'm stronger than I look and managed two resounding whacks on his buttocks with his face against the floor before he struggled out of reach. "Stop. I can explain, please." Cowards are bratty and come in all colors, languages and shapes, but it had been awhile since I'd encountered one.

Let *me* explain about exclusives. The rules are simple. The john leaves his wallet in sight, and I lock away his pants. There's a hand towel in the bathroom; towels for the shower are offered *after* money's crossed hands. It's a question of trust. No payment before services but no credit. Only once did a john walk out butt naked, before lunch, although he was certifiable. That was before I began checking references.

Hewitt was orally fixated—unusual for an exclusive the boy was *insatiable*—which meant I had not undressed. "So, talk."

"Could I, uh, put my pants on?" He couldn't hide the rise and blushed like the boy he was. It was as lame as Adam and the apple.

I glared.

He started talking quickly. "False pretences. I want to do a book about you, I mean with you. This," He waved at the air, "wasn't supposed to happen, but I couldn't help myself." He stopped, sheepishly wide-eyed, and turned a deeper shade of tomato. "You really are incredible, just like they all said."

Like I needed *him* to tell me. "A book? *This* is how you go about asking?"

"So will you do a book? Lewinsky sold over a million."

The comparison to an amateur riled. "She's hardly in my league. Anyway, what would I want to write about?"

"I write it. Your life of course." He winked slyly. "We could do a great exposé of your clientele and you'd never have to work again."

That was when I pulled the handgun and motioned him towards the door. "Out."

"But..."

"Now." I grabbed his clothes, briefcase, and cell phone, opened the door, and tossed them out. The dot.com that took up most of the floor cleared out nine months ago and their quarters were still vacant. It was unlikely anyone would be around.

He was about to object until I pointed the gun at his "precious stones."

"Okay, okay, I'm out."

Don't get this wrong, I'm not the violent type, but I don't believe in biting the hands that feed you. The gun's legal but I've never fired it except at a range. In my line, you'd be mad not to carry some insurance. I'm competent at martial arts as well.

Hewitt, however, had other ideas. Within minutes he was on his phone. "Don't hang up. I'll pay you, honest. I just didn't plan on... you know. I've got the cash, I'm getting it even as we speak."

He offered to buy me dinner. In Chinatown. "I'll spring for a limo, as long as you'll listen to my pitch. We could do a memoir-like novel, the kind we could sell for a movie deal? I'm well connected. If we do this right we could make a bundle."

Like I said, business was slow, and I was getting tired of the day job. It was awhile since I'd eaten in Chinatown, and I wanted my money. Plus I'd have nothing to lose by listening. There was something pathetically attractive about him. For all his cool, he had zero finesse. Like a virgin.

Over the week or so he "interviewed" me, he'd come up with wild scenarios of my fictionalized life. The kid was funny, and asked *tons* of questions. I liked telling him the more-or-less-real story of my life, although he asked mainly about my being Lady Day on Wall Street. I told, probably too much, although it didn't seem like it at the time. He "wrote" fast too. Every evening, he'd tape record our chats and by the next evening, he'd hand me maybe forty or more pages of "our novel" which I'd take home to bed. I'm not much of a reader anymore, except of financial news and such, but our book was fun to read. Besides, what with the war and all, business was bad so I had free time.

The idea, he claimed, was to spice things up and tell a story about a "China Doll Ring," using pieces of my life. "In the movie version," he said, "Michelle Yeoh could play the pimp and Gong Li her number one girl. What do you think?" I laughed at the idea of this dressed-up version of things. It all seemed unreal.

Truth is, Hewitt Chan made me laugh. Life's too short to cry, plus I could see he had the proverbial gun in his pocket most evenings, although he was a gentleman and a teetotaler. On the last night, I offered to comp him and the poor boy exploded in my mouth, *six times*. Sobriety, I guess. He didn't ask for anything else, and I assumed he was just scared, like many of the johns.

Anyway, when his *real* story hit the wires, exposing Kevin Leighton's financial shell game, I was livid. The little creep had said he had to go on a business trip and would see me in a week. Right. On the front pages of *The Wall Street Journal*. He did get a *non-fiction* book deal later to expand on the collapse of Leighton's empire, and in his book, he named Mahmoud and some of my best clients in a chapter about the "playthings" of oil men. Of course, before the book appeared, he published *that* chapter in *Esquire*, so it got this huge media splash. Such mendacity! The little creep embellished what little I told him, although all he had were composite johns, at best. As I said, when he tried to "interview" me for *those* kinds of details, I am paid to be discreet.

My only consolation is that he stiffed Bernard as well, that dumbass, the one who gave him the idea in the first place, *and* my number. Turns out Kevin and Mahmoud had never told him a thing about me, but Bernard did and told Hewitt who must have checked their schedules to figure out the best time to call. Bernard had the *nerve* to yell at me. There I was, *my* life's work coming undone, and he was worried about his reputation? Just before I hung up on him, I said that in future, he could damn well whip his own back.

So that's the story of Hewitt and why I've been lying low in Amsterdam. The joke of his "exposé" was how little he exposed, how he missed the real story because he was blinded by his own agenda, tricked by his expectations. Obviously, Bernard hadn't told him every-thing, and sometimes, I think about telling Hewitt the truth, just to give him a jolt. I started telling him about Chou-li once, and might have given away the whole game, but he stuck to his specific line of questioning. In the end, Hewitt was just a scam artist after the money, but not nearly as smart as he thought he was.

Did I forget to say that I specialize in oral pleasure and back door entry? You'd be amazed at how large the market niche is of hypo-crites, homophobes, and the maritally denied, the last being a cover for their true desires. Johns are predictable; for all their money, power, and bully-boy tactics, none of them can really face themselves. Which was how I could be her, Lady Day, the mistress of masquerade.

Penile agenesis. That's the medical name for my condition. I used to think of myself as one of a long line of Chinese eunuchs, the privi-leged house slaves of Beijing's royal concubines who lounged around with bound feet. It's entirely likely that at least a few eunuchs were born intersexuals, rather than castrated. My life might have been gender-specific if I hadn't been illegitimate, if I hadn't been sent away, if Ah Lum, my baby *amah*, my nursemaid, hadn't been the sweet, if sad, lady she was. If Daddy hadn't been a rich and powerful man. But *what if* doesn't make a life. *What is*, does.

So here's my life, which isn't a novel or a movie starring anyone, not even B.D. Wong, the actor who played such a brilliant butterfly girl on stage. When you're one in twenty million births, your story vanishes in the history of the world.

My name... but you don't need to know that, do you? I go by Lady Day Wai which is possibly my mother's name. She was mixed race—a Chinese-Pakistani journalist I think—who had a fling with Daddy; his name you'd recognize because it graces a publicly traded multinational headquartered in Hong Kong. When Daddy dictates, the world listens. I envy him that. A long time ago, I studied international lady journalists, and turned up one surnamed Wai who fit the bill, and so took that name. But I saw her on television later, and she looks nothing like me. Also, she worked for some Australian fashion magazine and it's unlikely she and Daddy would have met.

I only have Daddy's word for it—and my pale-chocolate pigmentation—that my mother really was who he said she was.

Did I say I'm gorgeous, stunningly, exotically beautiful? That I age slowly, despite my condition which sometimes results in premature osteoporosis, that I am the dream Asian seductress, complete with dark, smoldering, slanted eyes, cheeks with a peach-blossom blush, and lips as succulent as the reddest lychees?

Daddy. Sometimes, even now, I can still conjure him up, or rather, his suits. They were all so determinedly tailored. Cuffed pants, razor-sharp crease; rich wool or gabardine or silk blends; thin, black leather belts with brushed gold buckles. He usually stood during his brief visits, and since I was a small child, I spent most of those visits studying his crotch.

Daddy did not subject me to surgery at birth, which was the usual treatment for my condition back then, to refashion the unborn penis into a vagina. As for my mother, well, you forget about what never was—she did allow me life after all—and remember Ah Lum instead.

I was tutored at home—in everything from classical Chinese to Latin to the geography and history of the world, I was nothing if not well educated—and dressed as a boy whenever Daddy visited. But all my early life, I was Ah Lum's girl. She had a harelip that contorted her features so badly even I occasionally averted my gaze. She loved me though, fiercely, with the passion of one who recognizes and protects her tribe. She taught me control, the suppression of temper, and the power of a face that does not flinch.

On my eleventh birthday, I saw Daddy for the last time.

"You're going away to school," he said. He pulled off my cap and yanked at my too-long hair. "And we'll cut this off, properly."

I stared at his crotch. "Yes, *A-Ba*."

"Don't call me that. I am your uncle from now on, the brother of your mother who died in China. That's what you'll tell everyone." He said *uncle* in English and right then I felt I wouldn't see him again.

"Yes, uncle," I replied in English.

"You will go to boarding school, in England."

"Can Ah Lum come too?"

"You're too old for a baby *amah*. You know that, don't you?"

I kept quiet.

"Now I will show you something so that you can understand who you are." He gestured for Ah Lum to leave the room, and locked the door. "Here," he said, unzipping his pants and pulling out what towers in my memory as the tiniest penis in the world. "This is what you are. When you're grown up, your manhood will help you survive and run successful enterprises. I came here from China with nothing. Now I have sons, and wealth."

I stared at his shrimp-like thing, almost buried in his testicles, and wondered if he also sat to urinate, the way I did.

He zipped himself up and sat down, the one time I recall that he did. I stared at his face, the smooth, hairless chin, the thick lips that seemed permanently fixed in a scowl, the eyes that refused to look directly at me. "Even you," he said, "will not disgrace me. At least you are intelligent, and diligent. Learn to be independent. In the end, there is no one you can count on except yourself."

Years later, when all that was ancient history, I researched my father's family and learned he had another son, a couple of years younger than me, and a daughter. He still runs the company, because the son is a good-looking playboy, not terribly bright, who spends all his time fucking models and pop stars, globally gracing the gossip pages with his licentious and drunken behavior. In an interview published in *The Wall Street Journal* some years back, Daddy refers to an older son who died as a child, a responsible and intelligent boy. By then his alabaster-skinned Chinese wife was dead and could not tell.

Did I say that puberty was the most horrifying time of my life?

At boarding school, I wore a pair of fake glasses, pretending myopia, so that the more honorable boys wouldn't hit me. Being an A student, I bought safety through my enterprise, selling crib sheets with immaculately neat, hand-printed answers to exams that boys could hide without difficulty. I feigned illness to avoid physical activity, relying on the discretion and protection of the headmaster and doctor who knew, but exercised in secret to stay strong. But as voices deepened, and wet dreams sprayed the nights, I felt the encroaching danger of rampant masculinity, dogging me like a nightmare from which I couldn't awake. My Adam's apple did not bulge, and desire surfaced, but only within.

Linus Wu, the one other Chinese boy at the exclusive English enclave, arrived at the school when I was twelve. He was two years my senior, from some rich Chinese family in Singapore and fancied himself another Bruce Lee.

I was collating information for my enterprise one afternoon in the study room when he sauntered by in the company of his best friend, Gordon Littlefield.

"Hey, *Miss* Charlie Chan," Linus said, laughing at his own joke. "I need a literature crib sheet. Make me one."

I kept my head down. "That'll be two pounds. Those take extra work."

"What, no favors for your *dai go?*"

"You're not my brother."

He grabbed the back of my neck and squeezed it in a choke hold. "Do it, fairy, or I'll tell headmaster what you've been up to." Then, he released me, but not before banging my forehead against the table top.

"Now," he said. "I need that literature sheet, and Gordon needs one for chemistry. One pound for both. Have you got that?"

I mumbled. "Yes."

"Where are your manners?"

"Sirs."

They laughed their way out of the study room.

I prepared those sheets. My consolation was knowing how unintelligent they both were, because here I was, one form behind them, able to answer their exams.

Their demands grew. Within a couple of terms, I was virtually doing all their schoolwork, and supplying crib sheets for too many subjects. To keep me in check, they regularly played what they called their "game" with me. Gordon, who was clearly subordinate to Linus, would drag me out of bed in the middle of the night and force me to suck him till he came. Linus watched, and masturbated. Eventually, I had had enough. I was tired of being pushed around by those two and decided to teach them a lesson. Things, I reasoned, couldn't get any worse.

The success of my enterprise hinged on the fact that my crib sheets were imperfect. My customers needed to pass, which was not the same as getting As. Only Linus and Gordon demanded near-perfect grades, which was why they needed my full-time services for consistency. They may not have been the brightest, but they weren't idiots.

A midterm was coming up. I settled on the literature exam for my revenge. This required full-blown essays, and I had to write out several in advance on thin sheets of airmail paper which they could fold up into tiny squares to bring into the exam. That spring, I laughed myself silly over their essays, which I peppered with as many deliberately wrong statements as I dared. The red herring was the one that began, "In Shakespeare's comedy, *The Tempest*, King Lear is confronted with a dilemma. The queen had said of their daughters, *Let them eat cake*, which was meant as a treat, but Ophelia, the queen's rival for Lear's affection, poisoned the cake and all but the youngest girl died. Now, the queen wanted Ophelia executed, but the king was loath to kill his mistress." Neither one, I knew, had ever read a single Shakespearean play. I marked that sheet as a possible answer for a question on *The Tempest* or on the character of Lear, or on the comedies, knowing in advance that neither *The Tempest* nor Lear would be on the exam, and that they would likely use one of the two other compare-and-contrast essays I'd prepared for the comedies, since those were obviously more appropriate, not nearly as silly, and would garner, at worst, a C-minus, which is what Gordon got.

Who knew? Linus was just stupid enough.

His class, I heard, howled over the teacher's reading of that essay, for which Linus got an F. The boys who knew came and congratulated me afterwards; by then, those two had become a bullying pair no one liked. When Linus tried to confront me, everyone mocked him openly, and he left, red-faced and furious.

Linus Wu and Gordon Littlefield surrounded my bed that night. Gordon grabbed my glasses.

"Get up," he hissed. "We're going for a long walk."

"I'm not going," I said.

Linus slapped my face twice with both hands, hard. "What are you going to do, girl face? Scream?"

The two of them forced me out into the chill of an English spring. Under an elm by the playing field, they raped me in turn, for real. This was as much their virginal loss as it was mine, because they rushed clumsily through the proceedings, never turned me over, and consequently never saw my strange fruit. Yet through all that, I knew it was their awful lust, and not just the need for revenge, that truly propelled them. Before they left, Linus ground my glasses under his heel. "Tell and you're dead," he said.

I lay out in that open field for hours, refusing to cry, refusing to feel sorry for myself. I thought of Ah Lum, brushing and braiding my hair which grew long in between Daddy's visits, putting me in dresses with soft frills, showing me pictures of Chinese movie stars of the Forties with their crimped hair and rouged cheeks, bathing me with lavender soap, dusting me with rose-scented talcum powder. There was no one to blame, not even her, nor Daddy, for this mess I was in. What did I expect? I had my revenge all right, and this was the result. Eventually, I got up, shut out the pain, and found my way back to the dormitory where my assailants slept like rough logs. This was it. I had managed to hide my genitals till now and put up with the façade of boarding school, but the charade had to end before Wu and Littlefield subjected me to even worse torture. They weren't done with me yet, of that much I was certain. I was fourteen.

That weekend, I disappeared to London. Luckily, it was near the end of term, so a large bank draft had arrived. I withdrew all the money and bought myself girl's clothes, makeup, and a wig for until my hair grew out. In a public women's toilet, late at night when no one was around, I discarded my male garb and became "Girl-Girl."

Was I scared? Of course. Just because bodies were for sale all around me didn't mean I *wanted* this life. But there is a desperation so profound that it is beyond all feeling, beyond what we call our common humanity. Daddy wasn't wrong about my intelligence; I knew what survival meant. What is it Kevin says? Walk the walk; talk the talk. That's how you do it.

Nightlife is a blanket more secure than narcotics or drink. I stayed undercover, shopping around my eternal girlishness. English schoolgirl, China girl-child bride, lascivious Lolita. There wasn't a "Girl-Girl" I wouldn't play for those who really wanted a boy. Johns of all stripe lack imagination, and I had to keep the money coming in. Daddy had closed the bank account after my big withdrawal, just like that, and never even tried to look for me. I half expected it but

I cried that day, uncontrollably, frightened by this final, irrevocable severance, because a small part of me wanted to believe he loved me at least a little.

But I missed daylight, and school. A month after my transformation, I put on my girl's school uniform, without makeup, and passed the daylight hours at the British Library, reading whatever I could.

It was there that I met Chou-li. He's dead now, must be. He was already in his seventies then, surprisingly upright, which gives me a slender hope. I had seen him a few times in the reading room, always poring over the Chinese newspapers. Sometimes, he'd nod and wave. I couldn't help noticing his extremely long, exquisitely groomed nails. All his nails were long, not just the pinkies.

He sat opposite me one afternoon. I recall the shaft of sun between us, glistening with dust motes. His eyes were startlingly sharp, and I felt as if he stripped me with his gaze.

"Chinese?" He asked, in English.

I nodded. "Mostly."

"Do you speak?"

"*Ke-yi,*" I replied in Mandarin, because he looked northern.

He smiled. "*Ni bu shi nüxing de. Shi ma?*"

I wanted to bolt. How did this old man guess my questionable girlhood?

"Don't be afraid," he said, laying one hand on my arm. "I'm like you too. *Yan ren.*"

I didn't understand, having never heard the term in Chinese. He noted my confusion and said in English, "*Eunuch.* You understand? You too?"

Despite his gentle voice, I was frightened by his unrelenting gaze. "No, not me," I said in English, retreating to the safety of my by-then greater fluency.

"I see. Come with me?"

"Daddy wouldn't like it," I lied.

He cocked his head. "Really?"

I lowered mine, ashamed. "I have to make money."

"No," he said, leaning very close. "You don't have to, not yet. Follow me."

He stood up then and began to walk away, glancing back at me. "*Lai, lai,*" he urged. Come, come.

I shook my head and remain seated. He merely smiled, and left.

A few days later, I saw him again. He handed me an envelope filled with pound notes. "*Soonggeini.* Present." He saw me hesitate and added, "Go on, take it. Your daddy can't look after you forever."

I wanted to push it away, but couldn't. The night before, a john had hurt me so bad I was still bleeding in the morning, and he stiffed me. This time, I followed Chou-li to his enclave of transsexuals, transvestites, intersexuals, hermaphrodites, bisexuals, homosexuals. Many were foreign, from Asia and the Middle East, although there were one or two English. Chou-li had been a eunuch in the last Chinese court, or so he claimed. All I knew was, in this home, I had found my tribe.

He said, "You'll stay with me. You can be my boy." When I shook my head, adamant, he smiled. "Okay, girl," adding, "mistress."

And so for a time, I was his very precious daughter. He seemed to take pleasure in serving me, drawing my baths, arranging my meals, taking me anywhere in London I wanted to go. I *was* his "mistress" and he made me command, verbally, even physically, which I quickly discovered I had a knack for. I suspected he wasn't really rich, but he didn't seem to want for money. He took me regularly to doctors, to make sure no new complications had arisen. He tutored me in Chinese poetry and history, and took me to the library often, saying it was good to study. Once, I asked him about his castration, because he had told me it happened when he was five or six. He refused to talk about it. Then, I asked if he felt desire and he said that some things you know inside, undeniably, and nothing the world has wreaked in its inhumanity can ever take away the comfort of that knowledge. He had seen many naked women, and despite the men who raped him, he knew it was women he would have desired.

Most of all, he taught me what I needed to know about sex, as if he knew, somehow, that I could not escape the life. *Take charge,* he instructed. *That's how you'll be safe. Remember what I've taught you. Compromise only what you must. And always, always, whenever you can, reduce the risk.* The others in his home—a large, four-room flat that was always full—came and went, and I learned over time that almost all were prostitutes, escorts, or exotic dancers.

But even Chou-li couldn't look after me forever.

On my eighteenth birthday, I made my Atlantic crossing. Chou-li cried when I left, but he let me go, saying he had done all he could for me. He placed in my purse a sealed envelope of money, which he told me to use prudently. Afterwards, I saw that he had given me two thousand pounds. Daddy's wealth shriveled against Chou-li's magnanimity. I wept tears as sweet as those I'd shed over my parting from Ah Lum.

My first day john was a Wall Street lawyer, sometime in the Seventies. I was in my early twenties by then, and managing. "He wants it before breakfast," my transvestite pimp, Sarabella, said. "And he specifically asked for an Oriental, so I quoted double." I smiled and took the address. This was before Asian immigration flooded the market, which was why I expanded internationally in the early Nineties.

So this client—*Larry, or was it Michael?*—was behind his desk playing with himself when in I walked at five a.m. sharp. Punctuality matters, especially during the day when schedules are tight. Decent-looking, early fifties, Jewish, not overweight, he was new at this. I know because after the first one he said, "Is it slanted at all or what?" and tried to cop a feel. I slapped his hand, hard enough to sting, but kept the tone light. "Sorry, off limits," I said. "You know it's extra for that."

He offered coffee and donuts. I chose a cream-filled one to kill the bad taste. His was bitter and sour, and I wondered if he didn't have some kind of illness.

"Do you always come to work this early?" I asked. Sarabella

insisted we make conversation, to prove we were really an "escort service."

He replied. "My wife's leaving me. I sleep here sometimes."

"So there's a shower here?"

He pushed open the door behind his desk to an executive bathroom larger than the room I inhabited.

"Neat."

"You finished with that donut yet?"

I swallowed and crawled over. *Stay on your knees,* Sarabella said. *They like that.*

When he handed me the money I asked, "So why did you want an Oriental?"

"Because her fucking boyfriend is." He seemed embarrassed because he added, "Quit being nosy."

Exit, stage left, but as the sun rose over the Hudson, I couldn't help wondering why his wife had chosen an Asian, because I very nearly choked on this john. Not that *all* Asian men are... but Daddy, you know, and Linus Wu as well, for that matter. In my experience, Hewitt was a rare exception.

But he got me thinking about day jobs, because I *am* a morning person. The trade's less conspicuous by day. More business-like. In a commercial building, traffic during office hours is the norm. I could look like the rest of the world in sunlight, which ameliorated the compromise.

So I started my "BLCB & CS fund" with ten dollars of the payment from that first day john. You know, I can still wear the Chanel suit, which, with care, has lasted nicely over the years. A lightweight wool-silk blend, gray with pale red piping along the edge of the waist-length jacket, a shapely skirt split modestly at the knee, that suit was *made* for me. None of my later, tailored ones ever looked as good. The black leather clutch briefcase has given way to a larger, hard-shell version, one with a compartment for business accessories, although I sometimes still carry the original, instead of a purse, for effect.

A few years later I left Sarabella to work only daytime johns and built my solo enterprise. It was an amicable parting. She supplied "ladies" for evenings, and was happy to send customers my way. If I *must* work for someone, I do prefer women, real or otherwise, who are so much more organized than their male counterparts. Which is why I don't mind Madame here in Amsterdam. She's a transsexual who runs a long-established, high-class, global escort service for "special needs." I just don't care for the nightlife because you end up looking sleazy, even in designer, because it's what the clientele wants, because even those who need never become working girls have been seduced by fashion to ape the look.

War's supposed to be good for business. This one wasn't, but that probably has more to do with the economy. Revenue slid thirty percent. God-and-Allah-fearing leaders may or may not themselves be whoremongers, but the primary trick of their trade is to inspire the masses and maintain institutions. Crusades happen as long as there are men who want virgins, as Daddy once said. Surprising what sticks as the years roll along, like those odd Daddy-isms. Like Linus Wu and Gordon Littlefield.

This is getting complicated. All I meant to tell was about Hewitt and how he scammed me. Funny how telling one story leads to the next and the next.

That first dinner, Hewitt talked nonstop. He said he wanted to interview me and write a memoir, *fictionalized of course,* he emphasized, because he figured "we" could get a lot of money. The kid was smooth, pretty convincing what with his impressive list of contacts. At one point, he pulled out this file folder with business cards of executives in big publishing companies, and Hollywood as well. He described a potential story line, a way to disguise everyone. It would *not* be an exposé; we'd work as a team. "We," he kept saying.

"What do you say?" He asked when dinner was over. "Can I tell my publishers I have my source?"

I looked him in the eye. "You already have a contract?"

"Sure."

"Show me."

I can't be certain now, but it seemed he hesitated, and that should have tipped me off. He could probably tell I wasn't entirely sold. But he opened his case and pulled out a manila envelope right there and then and handed it to me.

"I brought you a copy," he said.

The printed return address read Harper Collins. I took the envelope, smoothed my skirt, and stood up. "I'll check it out. Thanks for dinner."

The kid was smarter than I gave him credit for because the contract was for a half-million-dollar advance, with an editor's name at Harper Collins. I verified the number with directory inquiry, called, and sure enough, this editor confirmed everything. Hewitt and I even signed a separate contract, giving me sixty-five percent of everything, but only because I insisted. I was happy, thinking I'd cut myself a great deal.

And then, the day his story appeared, everything stopped. There it was: "At the Office: From the Diary of a New York Call Girl." The more I read, the angrier I got. He blew my cover, even naming whose offices I used. Carter Mahmoud yelled so loudly over the phone that I completely lost my cool. I was shaking, crying. Me. Who knows better than to lose control. Kevin slammed the phone the last time I called. He'll likely end up in jail for a spell; the trial's still not over. I felt worst for him. He made me money, ensuring my longevity, my survival, even if he was a crook.

For whatever reason, Hewitt Chan kept my identity secret, never attempted to deliver me to the D.A. Exposure wouldn't have hurt, not the way it hurt the johns. What upset me, even more than the money, was that he never gave me the end of "our novel." Which is why I started reading books about the life. Turned out he'd "borrowed" my story from one about some Mayflower lady pimp (some of the chapters were verbatim—like I said, the wanton man lacks imagination). When I had pointed out I wasn't a pimp, he said, "details."

Who knew?

You know, you shouldn't believe those books. Most don't tell it like it really is. Some dress up the life, so that it's glamorous, racy, and salacious. Others are sob stories of unwilling victims or children of poverty, and manipulate your sympathies as shamelessly as pimps can. Trust me, I know. In the end, it's just a business like any other, and for me, as good a life as I was likely to get. One of highs and lows, of good days and bad, of profits and people, of liars and straight shooters, of sinners and martyrs and all those in between. There are no winners or losers in this awesome game, just buyers and sellers of whatever it is we humans must transact, as long as we're still in play.

Anyway, thanks to Hewitt, I disappeared for the second time in my life. Took my laptop, the gray Chanel plus a few other clothes, and left the country. With the war and all, there were inexpensively empty flights to Europe in first class. Also, the war has meant good profits on my currency contracts. At least this time I really can count on myself.

I should have known better, not been taken in by the scam, which is what irks me most. Hewitt planned everything so perfectly. Turned out the editor was his girlfriend—was *that* the brief hesitation?—and the document, false. Clearly, he was taking a risk, or rather his girlfriend was, but he had calculated, correctly, that I wouldn't raise a stink. I did think about doing so, for all of five seconds. The thing is, thanks to the likes of Kevin and Bernard, I knew when it was time to cut my losses.

But he got me thinking about Linus and Gordon, and about my own feebly planned scam that failed. I wasted so much energy writing those essays, getting caught up in the fiction, that I forgot about the *business* of revenge, that it should be final, and the avenger untouchable. I left myself wide open, and was forced to disappear for fear of further reprisals, ending my profitable enterprise in crib sheets, ending what last hope I had for a viable daylight life. I would like to say that Linus and Gordon and that time are all behind me, but some things stay inside, whether you want them to or not.

Which is why I did some diligent research and turned up a few interesting details of my own. That's how I came to work nights again, for Madame.

Linus Wu's a big shot now. He runs a telecommunication enterprise in China and travels all the time. Linus never married; he only fucks whores. Gordon Littlefield's a global venture capitalist in London with a trashy young wife who runs around, literally, with the raciest royals, cuckolding him publicly. Linus and Gordon are still best friends; we're comfortable with our tribe, I suppose. They both continue to indulge their "special needs"—I rather suspected they did—and have been Madame's clients for many, many years. They're quite inseparable. All the "girls" here know about them and wouldn't you know it, no one readily takes on the "dynamic duo" as they're known, even though they pay double for the pleasure and are reliable regulars. Trust me, it is a smaller world than we think and some things really don't change.

So I laid low for awhile, patiently working for Madame, studying the lay of the land, figuring that eventually, my day would come. I never told Madame my real story when we met, using a different name—risky, but I interviewed well—and offered myself for "B & B" transactions. It's been tedious, tying up johns, but I needed the bondage practice.

About six months ago, the perfect opportunity presented itself.

I had been watching their pattern. The two of them would show up, quarterly it appeared, hang out for a week, and call for girls three or four nights. I calculated that it might not be a good idea to take them on together right away, in case one recognized me. Each would also show up solo, Gordon quite regularly, and I decided it would be prudent to start with the subordinate. When Gordon called in alone that time, he wanted Kavali, this tiny Indian transvestite who specializes in bondage and Spanish fly transactions. Later, out of Madame's earshot, I pulled her aside and offered double his rate to substitute.

"Are you crazy?" she asked, taking the money. "How will you convince him it's okay?"

"Don't worry about that. I'll take care of things. You enjoy your night off."

He was wary at first, but bought my story about Kavali's "emergency." That first night, I didn't try to sell anything, and won trust by showing him such a good time so that he'd ask for me again. He had always been a big boy, but now he was portly and virtually impotent, which we fixed with Spanish fly, a mental rather than real aphrodisiac, and in his case, the bondage plus persuasive pandering seemed to be what really did the trick. What I remembered with clarity, what stuck over the years, was that whenever he was in ecstasy, he never seemed to feel pain, because I often used my teeth on him all those times during their "game" but he never once complained. His foreskin was thick and his penis unusually fat, which might have accounted for it, or else, he was unduly masochistic. He didn't recognize me at all, which I'd counted on, because Gordon was one of those boys who never looked beyond the end of his nose. He hadn't changed.

As I said, no one liked those two, so when I became Gordon's regular, Madame was relieved. By then, I'd proved I would deliver and could more or less be trusted. *Best practice,* as Bernard used to say in his professorial tones, *means satisfying the one who calls the shots.* As for customers, *you have to study the pattern of their needs.* The corollary is knowing the *immediate* need and delivering that before all else.

About a month ago, I had Gordon tied up in bed one night when I told him about a super-fly Viagra combo that had "just appeared on the market."

"It has to be injected though," I explained, loosening his mouth gag to let him speak. Sensing his trepidation, I added, "Some men are terrible cowards. You're not, darling, are you?" Earlier, I had given him what I said was the super-fly, in reality a Viagra, the kind that can cause the four-or-more-hour-erection side effect, to see how it affected him. An hour later, he was still in play but beginning to falter.

"Well," he said, "perhaps just a teensy weensy bit?"

As I said, johns are predictable. The Spanish fly ones always want more, and the trick is to exhaust them or spike their drinks so they sleep.

We did the injection. It worked like a charm. Procaine's an impressive substance.

Afterwards, I told him I wanted to take on his dynamic duo. He looked so pleased that I knew the deal would finally be sealed.

Tonight's their last night. The first evening, Linus wondered aloud why I seemed familiar, but I poured him more brandy, flashed my privates and said, *you wouldn't forget that easily, would you, darling,* allaying his suspicions.

Reduce the risk.

This time, I've planned properly, having learned a lesson from Hewitt. Had I been under Chou-li's tutelage sooner, I would never have pulled the stunt I did with those two all those years ago. *It's good to study,* Chou-li always said. *Yan ren,* castrated person. Chinese doesn't hide the meaning like English does with *eunuch.*

I've studied castration.

In Gordon's case, it's easy. He'll be tied up anyway and anesthetized, taken care off with the injection. Never was too intelligent, that boy, especially in the sciences. He used to follow my crib notes in chemistry lab to a T, one time creating a stink so bad the class was evacuated. When he complained, I pointed out how he'd confused a nitrate with a chloride. He mumbled something about my writing more clearly in future and never knew the difference. As for numbing him, he loved my biting him harder and harder, which I could do by progressively increasing the dosage. It's all part of the plan. I want him to watch.

Linus still likes to watch, which he did earlier this week while I serviced Gordon. The thing is, these days, he helps himself along with liquor, vast quantities of it. It's so typically Chinese, especially among the country-of-origin variety, making him inattentive and vulnerable. Surprisingly, the man didn't need artificial stimuli, although he fizzles out fast on entry. In any case, the old-fashioned Mickey Finn will do the job—a mild version—plus I'll tie him up and inject Novocain to prevent the pain reviving him. I've packed plenty of rubbing alcohol, gauze, bandages, and sutures along with the surgical blades. I'll do him first. It'll double Gordon's pleasure. Linus will know quickly enough because his knockout will last only as long as it takes to finish off Gordon. The pain will kick in within an hour or two, by which time I'll be off on a plane somewhere, dressed in timeless Chanel.

Strange fruit, perhaps, but we needn't remain hanging "from the poplar trees."

Time we ripened, don't you think?

Oh I forgot to say that some of Lady Day's most informative, and *helpful,* clients belong to the medical profession. Surprising how much you can learn from books.

After tonight, I'll finally be done with the life. My one regret is that Madame will lose two of her best clients, although I will send a money order for the entire transaction, instead of just her commission. A small price to pay for severance. I *don't* like to bite the hand that's fed me, but this is business after all and nightlife has its risks. The bottom line? She'll always have fresh johns.

Daylight again. Soon.

Lightning Source UK Ltd.
Milton Keynes UK
UKOW03f1521140214

226486UK00008B/307/P